Great Expectations

A play

Hugh Leonard

Adapted from the novel by Charles Dickens

Samuel French — London
New York - Toronto - Hollywood

GREAT EXPECTATIONS

First presented at the Gate Theatre, Dublin, on the 30th
November 1995, with the following cast:

Pip	Peter Gowen
Herbert Pocket	Eanna Breathnach
Young Pip	Simon Mulholland
Estella	Alison McKenna
Joe Gargery	Owen Roe
Magwitch	John Kavanagh
Mrs Joe/Biddy	Donna Dent
Pumblechook	Tom Hickey
Jaggers	Bill Golding
Miss Havisham	Susan Fitzgerald
Wemmick	Robert O'Mahoney
Molly/Miss Skiffins	Elizabeth Bracken
Aged Parent	Terence Orr

Directed by Alan Stanford
Designed by Bruno Schwengl
Lighting by Rupert Murray

CHARACTERS

Herbert Pocket: *twenty-three*
Pip: *twenty-three*
Young Pip: *fifteen*
Estella
Joe Gargery
Magwitch
Mrs Joe/Biddy: *to be played by the same actress*
Pumblechook
Miss Havisham
Jaggers
Wemmick
Molly
Miss Skiffins
Aged Parent: *Wemmick's father*
Villagers

The action of the play takes place in various settings in London and Kent

Period — Early nineteenth century

ADAPTER'S NOTE

The "look" of the play, including the stage setting, is of course a matter for the designer. However, the adapter sees three separate areas, thematic as well as spatial. In his mind's eye, the area stage left is Joe's World: the forge, the kitchen, the marshes (or "meshes") and the churchyard. To the right is Pip's World: this is London; the rooms Pip shares with Herbert, Jaggers' office and home, Wemmick's "castle" in Walworth. In the centre, raised, and connected to the rest of the stage by stairs, is Miss Havisham's world; this is thematically a kind of half-way house, a door leading from one world to the other.

There are two Pips, not for reasons of stagecraft, but because there are two in Dickens' book: the country boy and the young man he becomes. I have tried to reflect this duality by doubling some of the other parts and by stressing the double life of that delightful schizophrenic, Wemmick. There is one anachronism which is deliberate. The action of the book occurs no later than 1830, and my use of the word "snob" anticipates itself by ten years. Any other solecism is, as Dr Johnson observed when asked why he referred to the knee of a horse as the pastern, "Ignorance, Madam, pure ignorance."

Those who want an image of the characters as visualized by Dickens should of course go to the novel itself. However, I have found that often an actor who looks nothing like the author's description can still embody the nature and essence of a character to perfection. In choosing not to describe the people of the play, I make an exception in the case of Wemmick. Dickens' thumbnail portrait so exactly matches my own mental picture that I felt there could be little physical leeway. Of course, one could be wrong!

Hugh Leonard

Other plays by Hugh Leonard published by Samuel French Ltd

Da
A Life
Mick and Mick
Moving
The Patrick Pearse Motel
Pizzazz
Suburb of Babylon
Summer

PART I

PROLOGUE

Scene 1

London

The Lights come up R. We hear London street noises. Pip and Herbert Pocket are coming from the theatre. They are twenty-three. Their clothes are as befit young gentlemen of fashion. Their speech is rather affected, aping the current mode

Herbert My dear Handel, I declare in my life I never saw such acting.
Pip My dear Herbert, nor did I!
Herbert They do say he took America by storm.
Pip Small wonder. I confess that when his daughter, the unhappy Ophelia, was hanged ——
Herbert I believe her name was Cordelia. Pray forgive me for mentioning it.
Pip My dear Herbert, you do me a service.
Herbert My dear Handel, not at all.
Pip Well, I quite shared the King's dismay. And next week Mr Macready is to appear in "The Lady of Lyons". (*He pronounces Lyons as "lions"*)
Herbert The word, I believe, is (*correct pronunciation*) "Lyons". Don't reproach yourself, my dear fellow.
Pip My dear fellow, I shall not.
Herbert From the dawn of time the French, a deplorable race, have such an envy of us that they mispronounce the names of their cities for no better reason than to enable British travellers *"to lose"* their way.

During the following, Young Pip appears. He is fifteen and wears his Sunday best, country style

Pip Well, however you pronounce the wretched word, and if Macready is playing, we must at all costs —— (*He catches sight of Young Pip*)
Herbert We dare not miss it, my dear Handel. We should be beyond the pale, quite out of the fashion. We ... I say?

Pip It's that chap again.
Herbert The one who follows you? (*He turns to look*)

Young Pip moves into the shadows

Where? You, sir, show yourself!
Pip He's afraid of you. You face him, and he runs away. It is not you he has
business with.
Herbert Business? My dear, Handel, you have been in London for long
enough to know that beggars are under one's feet like cobblestones.
Pip If a beggar is what he is, why does he not beg?
Herbert Come, my dear fellow, our poor lodgings are to have a visitor.

*This is not naturalism; what Herbert is saying is that it is time for the next
scene*

SCENE 2

*The Lights cross-fade to Pip's and Herbert's lodgings. Young Pip remains
in the shadows*

Estella enters

Pip Estella!
Estella Can I believe my eyes? Are you Pip? Is it you?
Pip I believe that is the first time you have called me by my name.
Estella Is it? Then mark it down to astonishment. Where is the common boy
with whom I played cards and who called the knaves jacks? And I can see
that since your change of fortune and prospects you have not been slow to
change your companions.
Herbert You are kind enough to notice me. How are you, Estella?
Estella I am well. (*To Pip*) You and Herbert under the same roof!
Pip It was at Mr Jaggers' suggestion.
Estella Ah! Always Mr Jaggers!
Pip Mind, I had no notion that I was destined to share rooms with none other
than ——
Herbert ——than the pale young gentleman. That was his name for me in Miss
Havisham's garden the day Handel said:
Pip "Good-afternoon". And Herbert said:
Herbert "Come and fight!"
Estella Handel? Who, pray, is Handel?
Pip Why, I am.
Herbert You see, once he was a humble farrier, a bootmaker for
horses ——

Pip I was a blacksmith.
Herbert — and there is a charming piece of music by Handel, "The Harmonious Blacksmith", I thought: what more apt as a familiar name!

They laugh

Yes, I said "Come and fight" and I gave him the most fearful trouncing.

Estella exchanges a smile with Pip

Estella Oh, yes?
Pip But now we are the best of friends.

Joe enters

Joe (*to Young Pip*) Which I meantersay, Pip old chap, old fellow, ever the best of friends!

Joe and Young Pip exit

Herbert May I be excused? I do believe that Handel tells me with his eyes that I should be elsewhere.
Estella Does he! And I tell you with my words that you should stay. (*To Pip*) Tomorrow I am to go to live, at great expense, with a lady at Richmond who has the power of taking me about and showing people to me and showing me to people. The distance is ten miles. I am to have a carriage and you are to take me. I shall be here at nine, sharp. You are to take care that I have tea, and then we go to Richmond.
Pip That is Miss Havisham's wish?
Estella And mine.
Pip I do wonder that Miss Havisham can do without you.
Estella It is part of her plan for me. You know what she is for making plans. Until tomorrow then. Goodbye, Herbert.

Estella exits

Herbert Can you see me, then? I hardly thought I was visible.
Pip My dear Herbert, I have something very particular to say to you.
Herbert My dear Handel, I shall esteem and respect your confidence.
Pip Herbert — I love, I adore Estella.
Herbert (*easily*) Exactly. Well?
Pip "Well?" Is that all you say?
Herbert What next, I mean? Of course I know that.

Pip I never told you.

Herbert Told me? You have never told me when you have got your hair cut, but I have had senses to perceive it. You brought your adoration and your portmanteau here together.

Herbert exits

Pip So I did. I have never left off adoring her. And if I adored her before, I now doubly adore her. I think my life began on the day I first saw her. Or, rather not long before. My father's family name being Pirrip, and my christian name Philip (*his voice becomes that of a narrator*) my infant tongue could make of both names nothing longer or more explicit than Pip. So, I called myself Pip and came to be called Pip. (*He moves to the side of the stage*)

ACT I
The Convict

SCENE 1

Country

The Lights cross-fade to a graveyard in the country area L

Fog swirls in

Young Pip enters and kneels beside a grave

Pip The bleak place overgrown with nettles was the churchyard.

Young Pip Philip Pirrip, late of this parish, also Georgiana wife of the above ——

Pip —— were dead and buried, and ——

Young Pip —— Alexander, Bartholomew, Abraham, Tobias and Roger——

Pip —— infant children of the aforesaid, were also dead and buried, and the small bundle growing afraid of the churchyard and the river and the marshes and the sea beyond: that small bundle was ——

Young Pip —— was Pip.

Magwitch appears, all in coarse grey, with a great iron on his leg. He starts up with a terrible long-drawn-out cry of rage and hurtles himself across the stage

Magwitch seizes Young Pip by the throat. Young Pip screams

Magwitch Hold your noise. Keep still, you little devil, or I'll cut your throat.
Young Pip Oh, don't cut my throat, sir. Pray don't do it.
Magwitch Tell us your name. Give it mouth. Quick.
Young Pip Pip. Pip, sir.
Magwitch Show us where you live. P'int out the place.
Young Pip There, sir.
Magwitch You young dog, what fat cheeks you got. Damn me if I couldn't eat 'em.
Young Pip I most sincerely hope you won't, sir.
Magwitch Now, lookee here. Where's your mother?
Young Pip (*pointing to the gravestone*) There, sir.

Magwitch starts, makes to run and stops

No, sir. There. Next to my father, who's late of this parish.
Magwitch Ha. Who d'ye live with, supposin' you're kindly let to live, which I han't made up my mind about?
Young Pip My sister, sir. Mrs Joe Gargery, wife of Joe Gargery, the blacksmith, sir.
Magwitch Blacksmith, eh?

Magwitch looks at his leg-iron, then seizes Young Pip and puts his face up against the boy's

Now lookee here, the question being whether you're to be let to live. You know what a file is?
Young Pip Yes, sir.
Magwitch And you know what wittles is?
Young Pip Vittles, sir? Yes, sir.

Magwitch bends Young Pip backwards

Magwitch You get me a file. And you get me wittles. Or I'll have your heart and liver out. You hear me?
Young Pip Yes, sir, but if you would kindly please to let me keep upright, sir, perhaps I could attend more.
Magwitch You bring a file and wittles to me here, tomorrow mornin' early. Or else your heart and liver shall be roasted, tore out and ate. Now I ain't alone, as you may think I am. There's a young man hid with me, in comparison with which young man I am a angel. That young man has a secret way, pecooliar to himself, of getting at a boy, and at his heart and at his liver. A boy may lock his door, may be warm in bed, may draw the clothes over his head, may think himself safe, but that young man will

softly creep and creep his way to him and tear him open. Now what do you
say?
Young Pip I say that I shall most happily oblige you, sir.
Magwitch And Lord strike you dead if you don't.
Young Pip That too, sir.
Magwitch Then remember what you've undertook. Now get you home,
boy.
Young Pip Yes, sir. Good-night, sir.
Magwitch Much o' that! I wish I was a frog. Or a eel.

Magwitch shuffles away

SCENE 2

The Lights cross-fade to the Gargerys' house

Young Pip goes into the Gargerys' house

Joe enters

Joe Oh, Pip, Mrs Joe has been out a dozen times looking for you. And she's
out now, making it a baker's dozen.
Young Pip Is she, Joe?
Joe What's worse, she's got Tickler with her. She made a grab at Tickler and
she ram-paged out. That's what she did. She ram-paged out. On the Ram-
page, Pip, and off the Ram-page, Pip: such is life!
Young Pip So it would seem, Joe.
Mrs Joe (*off*) Pip!
Joe And now from what I can hear, Pip, she's come ram-pagin' back again.

*Mrs Joe comes in, carrying "Tickler", a thin cane. She takes hold of Young
Pip*

Mrs Joe So ... there you are. Where have you been?
Young Pip Only to the churchyard.
Mrs Joe (*flailing at him with the cane*) To the churchyard? If it wasn't for me,
you'd have been to the churchyard long ago and stayed there. Bench!

Young Pip kneels, his upper body over the bench

Who brought you up by hand?
Young Pip You did.

Mrs Joe beats Young Pip

Mrs Joe And why did I do it, I should like to know?
Young Pip I don't know.

Mrs Joe beats Young Pip again and flings him at Joe

Mrs Joe I don't! I'd never do it again. It's bad enough to be a blacksmith's wife, and him a Gargery, without being father and mother to you as well. Table!

This is a command that Joe and Young Pip should sit at table for their evening meal, which they do. Mrs Joe takes a loaf of bread, jams it against her bib, slaps butter on it as if applying a plaster and then saws thick slices for Young Pip and Joe

Young Pip (*in an undertone*) Joe ...
Joe Hallo, Pip.
Young Pip If you please, what is it to be brought up by hand?
Joe I don't rightly know, old chap.
Young Pip Nor do I. I ask, because I have wondered if perhaps Mrs Joe, being that way inclined, might have married you by hand.

Mrs Joe slaps down the slices of bread in front of Young Pip and Joe

Mrs Joe You may well whisper, you two betrayers and conspirers. Churchyard, indeed! You'll drive me to the churchyard betwixt you, one of these days, and oh, a pr-r-recious pair you'd be without me! Paupers, both of you. Me dead and you ——

There is a sound of distant cannon fire

Joe There, now. Hark to that.
Young Pip What is it, Joe?
Joe That's the gun they fire for warning, Pip. To say there's a conwict off.
Young Pip Off? Off where, Joe?
Mrs Joe Escaped, escaped!
Joe Dead o' winter, out on these meshes — poor fellow-creatur ...
Young Pip Who is? And who was firing, Joe?
Mrs Joe Ask no questions, you'll be told no lies.

Joe gives Young Pip a look that begs him not to aggravate Mrs Joe

Young Pip If you please, Mrs Joe, I should like to know, if you wouldn't much mind, where the firing comes from.
Mrs Joe From the Hulks.

Young Pip Hulks?
Joe 'Ulks.
Mrs Joe Sit!
Young Pip And, if you please, what's Hulks?
Mrs Joe Hulks is prison ships, right 'cross the meshes. The people in the
    Hulks are put there because they murder and rob and do all sorts of bad, and
    they always start off by asking questions.
Young Pip Do they?
Mrs Joe Eat. (*She turns away to attend to her own food*)

*Joe begins to chew slowly on his doorstep of bread. Young Pip, finding
himself unobserved, thrusts his bread inside his shirt. After a moment, Joe
stares at him*

Joe Pip, old chap. You'll do yourself a mischief. You can't have chawed it,
    Pip.
Mrs Joe What is it now?
Joe I say, you know. If you can cough any trifle on it up, Pip, I'd recommend
    you to do it. Manners is manners, but still your 'ealth's your 'ealth.
Mrs Joe You staring great stuck pig, I asked you what's the matter?
Joe (*to Mrs Joe*) Nothin'! Old chap, I bolted myself when I was your age,
    and as a boy I've been among many a bolter, but I never see your bolting
    equal yet, Pip, and it's a mercy you ain't bolted dead.
Mrs Joe What? Been bolting his food, has he? It's tar-water for you, my lad.
    Come and be dosed.

*Mrs Joe drags Young Pip from the bench on which he is sitting. She holds his
head under her arm, then takes up a large bottle and pours a copious dose
down his throat. Pip observes this*

Pip (*to the audience*) Some medical beast had revived tar-water in those days
    as a fine medicine. At the best of times, so much of this elixir was
    administered to me as a choice restorative that I was conscious of going
    about smelling like a new fence.
Joe Which I meantersay, Pip, you and me is always friends, and I'd be the
    last to carry tales and tell upon you, any time.
Mrs Joe (*releasing Young Pip to Joe*) Now you.
Joe Me, Pip?
Mrs Joe There's them as has bolted. And again, there's them as has seen them
    as has bolted. You'll have had a turn.

Joe runs out with Mrs Joe following

(*As she goes*) Gargery!

SCENE 3

Young Pip picks up some bread, cheese, a pork pie and a bottle of brandy and comes forward

The Lights cross-fade to the graveyard

Pip (*to the audience*) That night in my dreams a pirate called out to me from the gibbet station that I had better come and be hanged there at once. When the black sky outside my window was shot with grey, I went downstairs, and every crack in every board called after me "Stop, thief!" and "Get up, Mrs Joe!" I stole some bread and a rind of cheese and a pork pie. I stole brandy, and used a jug to fill the bottle up again. And I stole a file.

Young Pip goes to where Magwitch is waiting. Magwitch seizes the bread and the brandy. He eats, tearing the bread like an animal and takes a draught of the brandy

The Lights brighten to indicate dawn breaking. A church bell tolls

Young Pip awkwardly, shyly, extends a hand. Magwitch stares at Young Pip and the proffered hand, then wipes his own hand on his jacket and stiffly, almost formally, performs the handshake. It is not "Dickensian" sentiment: rather, it is a surreal bonding, an epiphany

  (*To the audience*) It was Christmas morn!

There is a great joyous pealing of bells that seems to fill the sky, and an impression of lightsomeness

The sound of the bells dies down. As it does so ——

SCENE 4

The Lights cross-fade to the Gargerys' house

Mrs Joe joins Young Pip. Uncle Pumblechook arrives from "outside" with a bottle each of sherry and port wine

Young Pip Mrs Joe! Mrs Joe! It's Uncle Pumblechook!
Mrs Joe Gargery! It's Uncle Pumblechook!
Pip (*to the audience*) Uncle Pumblechook was Joe's uncle, but Mrs Joe had appropriated him. And every Christmas Day he presented himself, as a profound novelty, with exactly the same words and carrying the two bottles, like dumbells.
Pumblechook Mrs Joe! I have brought you as the compliments of the season ... I have brought you, Mum, a bottle of sherry wine, and I have brought you, Mum, a bottle of port wine.
Mrs Joe Oh, Un-cle Pum-ble-chook, this is kind.

Pumblechook It's no more than your merits. (*To Young Pip*) And now are you all bobbish, and how is sixpenn-orth of ha'pence?
Mrs Joe Chair!

As instructed, Young Pip gives Pumblechook a chair

He's been down to hear the carols. I'm rather partial to carols myself, and, I daresay that's the best reason for my never hearing any. Me being — as Gargery would tell you, Uncle Pumblechook, if he had either the wit or the by-your-leave to speak out, which he han't — me being a blacksmith's wife and, what's the same thing, a slave with her apron never off.
Pumblechook Which goes to prove; be grateful, boy, to them which brought you up by hand.
Mrs Joe Huh! The young are never grateful.
Pumblechook Oh, naturally wicious, Mum. Naturally wicious.
Mrs Joe Gargery, are you set on standing there till New Year's? Uncle Pumblechook has come two mile across the meshes. Is he to have a glass of brandy or is he to die of cold?

Joe fetches the brandy bottle and pours a glass for Pip. Young Pip is dismayed. Pip speaks his thoughts

Pip (*to the audience*) Brandy. In the dark, how much water had I put in it? Would he find it weak? Would he say that it was weak?
Pumblechook He's been more trouble to you, Mum, than you would hear in a lenten sermon.
Mrs Joe Trouble! When I think of all the high places that boy has tumbled out of and all the low places he's tumbled into, and all the times, for his own good, I wished him in his grave, and he was too contrairy to go there ——
Pumblechook (*taking the brandy, holding the glass to the light*) Ah ... most hospitable. I wish you, the very merriest of Christmases, Mum, and again the season's compliments.
Mrs Joe Bless you ——

Mrs Joe pinches Joe

Joe
Mrs Joe } (*together*) — Uncle Pumblechook.

Pumblechook throws back his head and drinks the brandy off. He at once goes into a choking paroxysm

Mrs Joe Why, Uncle Pumblechook...?
Pumblechook Ta ... ta ... ta ...

Joe I think he be saying "thank-ee".
Pip (*to the audience*) Tar-water!
Pumblechook Tar-water!
Joe Tar?
Mrs Joe Tar?
Pumblechook Tar!
Mrs Joe (*looking from Joe to Pumblechook*) But how on earth? How in this
   world could the tar-water have gotten into the b ...? Pip! (*She looks now at
   Young Pip*)

*Young Pip, with a moan and a great histrionic gesture, stages a dead faint.
The others stare at him*

We hear the whoosh and crack and splutter of first one rocket, then another

Young Pip Another convict?
Joe That b'an't the firing of cannon. Them's rockets for a signal to the 'Ulks
   to send a boat. They got him. They've been and captured him.

The Lights fade on the Gargery home

SCENE 5

A Light comes slowly up on Magwitch, now in heavy chains and manacles

Joe and Young Pip move into this area

Pip, Mrs Joe and Pumblechook remain in the shadows

Magwitch Afore I set foot on that there vessel, I wish to say words respecting
   this escape. It may prevent some persons laying under suspicion alonger
   me, I stole some broken wittles up at the willage over yonder, and I'll tell
   you where from. From the blacksmith's.
Joe From the ...?
Magwitch It were some broken wittles, and a pie and a dram of liquor.
Joe Hallo, Pip!
Magwitch (*his glance seems to fall on Joe and Young Pip*) And I would say
   to that blacksmith, if he was here, I'm sorry to say, I would say to him, I've
   drunk your liquor and I've eat your pie.
Joe (*blurting out*) And God knows, you're welcome — (*he remembers
   himself*) so far as it was ever mine to give. And no-one the worse off, Pip,
   save maybe poor old Pumblechook. We wouldn't have you starve,
   miserable fellow-creatur, would us, Pip?

Magwitch turns away with no further sign and shuffles into the dark

Young Pip lingers to watch

The Lights come up in the kitchen. Mrs Joe serves something to Pumblechook

Pumblechook Thankee Mum! Most hospitable.

The Lights fade in the kitchen, leaving an area lit DS

Pumblechook stays in the shadows; Mrs Joe exits

SCENE 6

Pip (*to the audience*) It was impossible to mark the time of day, or for that matter the time of year, from the conversations between Joe and myself, for come rain or summer sun, the words, at least on Joe's part, were the slaves neither of time nor of fashion. In short, they were for ever the same.

Joe Pip, old chap, as you know, your sister is much given to government.

Young Pip Is she, Joe?

Joe Which I meantersay, the government of you and myself.

Young Pip Is it spring now, Joe?

Joe Which it are, old chap, seeing as how there's leaves on the trees and foals for the shoeing of. Which I never was no hand with calendars.

Young Pip Didn't you ever go to school, Joe?

Joe Well, Pip, I'll tell you. My father, Pip, he were given to drink, and when he were overtook with drink he hammered at my mother and me most onmerciful. He hammered at us with a wigour only to be equalled with the wigour with which he didn't hammer at his anvil. Well, someone must keep the pot biling or the pot won't bile. So I went to work, and that were a drawback on my learning.

Young Pip And is your father dead now, Joe?

Joe Which he went off in a purple leptic fit, Pip. And I had it put on his tombstone: "Whatsumever the failings on his part, Remember, reader, that he were good at heart. "

Young Pip If you say so, Joe.

Joe Which I do old chap. I were but lonesome for a while, living alone, so I got acquainted with your sister, who is a fine figure of a woman.

Young Pip I am glad you think so, Joe.

Joe I am glad I think so, Pip. A little redness or a little matter of bone here or there, what does it signify to me?

Young Pip Not at all, Joe.

Joe And if candour compel fur to admit that when on the ram-page she is a
  Buster, Pip, then it must also be said that your sister is a mastermind. Do
  you know what a mastermind is, Pip?
Young Pip No, Joe. What is a mastermind, then?
Joe Why, it is your sister. That's what it is.

SCENE 7

The Lights cross-fade back to the kitchen

Uncle Pumblechook is eating

Pumblechook (*calling*) They're here, Mum.

  Mrs Joe enters

Mrs Joe Now! If this boy an't grateful this night, he never will be. It is only
  to be hoped that he won't be Pompeyed.
Pumblechook Pampered, Mum? She's an't that sort, Mum.
Mrs Joe (*to Joe*) Well? What are you gawpin' at?
Joe Which some individual mentioned "she".
Mrs Joe And she is a she, I suppose? Unless you call Miss Havisham a he?
Joe Miss Havisham up town?
Mrs Joe Is there a Miss Havisham down town?
Pumblechook Good, Mum! Good indeed!
Mrs Joe Sit. You!

Joe attempts to sit

  Not you! Did I say that you might sit? (*She refers to Pip*) Him! Him! Him!
  Miss Haversham wants a boy to go and play there. And he had better play
  there, or I'll work him.
Joe Well, I wonder how she come to know Pip?
Mrs Joe Noodle! Who said she knew him?
Pumblechook Good, Mum. Well pointed!
Mrs Joe Isn't it just possible that Uncle Pumblechook is a tenant of hers?
  And couldn't she ask Uncle Pumblechook if he knew of a boy to go and
  play there? And couldn't Uncle Pumblechook, being ever considerate and
  thoughtful for us, mention this boy that I have forever been a willing slave
  to?
Pumblechook Good again! Prettily put. Now, Joseph, you know the case.
Mrs Joe And what Joseph does not know is that Uncle Pumblechook has
  offered to take the boy into town tonight in his own chaise-cart and to

deliver him with his own hands to Miss Havisham tomorrow morn. And Lor-a-mussy me! Here I stand talking to a mere mooncalf with, for all I know, my little brother's fortune to be made. Bucket!

Mrs Joe takes Young Pip by the ear, propels him to where there is a basin and goes through the business or the mime of scrubbing his face and neck

Pip (*to the audience*) At which, I was soaped and kneaded and towelled and thumped and harrowed and rasped. I may say that I own myself better acquainted than any living authority with the effect of a wedding ring passed unsympathetically over the human countenance. That evening, I was conveyed in the Pumblechookian chaise-cart and slept in a Pumble-chookian bed. Next morning ...

ACT II
Satis House

Scene 1

The Lights cross-fade to the exterior of Miss Havisham's house

Mrs Joe and Joe exit

A jangling bell is heard

Estella, now as a girl, appears holding keys

Pumblechook Boy, be for ever grateful to all friends, but especially unto them which brought you up by hand. (*To Estella*) Name of Pumblechook. And this is ... ah, Pip.
Estella Is it? Then come in, Pip. Did you wish to see Miss Havisham?
Pumblechook If Miss Havisham wished to see me.
Estella Ah, but you see she don't.

We hear the sound of heavy gates closing

Pumblechook Oh! Naturally vicious!
Estella (*to Young Pip*) Do you know the name of this house, boy?
Young Pip It's on the gate, Miss. (*Pronouncing it "saytis"*) Satis House, miss.
Estella The word is (*sahtis*) Satis, ignorant boy. It is Greek or Latin or Hebrew or such, and it means "enough".
Young Pip Enough House is a curious name, miss.

Estella It meant that whoever had this house could want nothing else. They must have been easily satisfied in those days, I should think. Don't loiter, boy.

Pip and Estella enter the house

Pumblechook exits

Jaggers appears. He is lighting his way with a candle

Jaggers And whom have we here?
Estella A boy.
Jaggers Boy of the neighbourhood? Hey?
Young Pip Yes, sir.
Jaggers (*taking Young Pip's chin between his fingers*) How do you come here?
Young Pip Miss Havisham sent for me, sir.
Jaggers Well! Behave yourself. I have a pretty large experience of boys, and you're a bad set of fellows. Now mind … you behave yourself!

Jaggers exits

Estella leads Young Pip to the top of the stairs

Estella There. Go in.
Young Pip After you, Miss.
Estella Don't be ridiculous, boy.

Estella exits, leaving Pip alone. He stands in the dark and quite alone

SCENE 2

Miss Havisham comes into view. She is seated on a throne-like chair with lighted candles around her. There is a small dressing-table by her elbow, containing dried flowers, jewels and a prayer book and with a pack of cards and a cloth-covered mirror on it. She wears a wedding dress, mouldering and about to fall apart

Young Pip (*speaking into the dark*) If you please… (*Louder*) If you please ——
Miss Havisham Who is there?
Young Pip Me, ma'am. Pip, ma'am. Mr Pumblechook's boy, come to play.
Miss Havisham Come nearer. Let me look at you. Come.

Pip does as he is bid, avoiding her eyes

Lift your eyes. Look at me. You are not afraid of a woman who has never seen the sun since you were born?

Young Pip No, ma'am.

Miss Havisham I think you are afraid. (*She lays her hands, one upon the other, on her left breast*) Do you know what I touch here?

Young Pip Yes, ma'am.

Miss Havisham What do I touch?

Young Pip Your heart, ma'am.

Miss Havisham Broken!

There is a pause

Young Pip If you say so, ma'am.

Miss Havisham I sometimes have sick fancies, and I have a sick fancy that I should like to see some play. So play. I have done with men and women. Play, play, play!

Young Pip looks embarrassed

What ails you? Are you sullen and obstinate?

Young Pip No, ma'am. I am very sorry for you, and I would do it if I could, but it's so new here and so strange and so fine ... and melancholy.

Miss Havisham So new to him, so old to me; so strange to him, so familiar to me. So melancholy to both of us. Call Estella.

Young Pip hesitates

You can do that. Speak Estella's name. Call her.

Estella hears her name and heads up the stairs

Young Pip moves to Estella

Estella Be silent. My name is not for your lips, boy. (*She goes to Miss Havisham*)

Miss Havisham takes up a piece of jewellery from the dressing table

Miss Havisham Come to me. Now. Where does this jewel shine the brightest, do you say? Against the dark of your hair (*she holds the jewel against Estella's hair*) or here, upon the whiteness of your skin? (*She holds the jewel against Estella's dress*)

Estella watches Young Pip, coquettishly gauging the effect of this little scene upon him

Estella My skin here is not uncovered.
Miss Havisham It will be when this is yours, my dear.
Estella When will that be?
Miss Havisham Have patience.
Estella When?
Miss Havisham One day, and you will use it well. Now let me see you play
  cards with this boy.
Estella No. He is a common labouring-boy.
Miss Havisham (*whispering*) What of it? You can break his heart.
Estella (*still child enough to be taken with the idea*) Can I? Shall I? (*She
  laughs and picks up the pack of playing cards from the dressing-table*)
  What do you play, boy?
Young Pip Nothing but "Beggar My Neighbour", miss.
Miss Havisham There! You can beggar him!

Young Pip and Estella sit at Miss Havisham's feet. Estella deals the cards contemptuously. They play during the following

Pip (*to the audience*) Estella won that game, and the next, while Miss
  Havisham sat and watched. There are bodies, buried in ancient times,
  which fall to powder in the moment of being distinctly seen. Had the
  natural light of day shone upon her, would she too have been struck to dust?

Young Pip deals the cards during the following

Estella He calls the knaves jacks, this boy. And what coarse hands he has.
  And what thick boots.

Young Pip fumbles with the cards

  And how stupid and clumsy he is.
Miss Havisham She says many hard things of you, but you say nothing of
  her. What do you think of her?
Young Pip I don't like to say.
Miss Havisham Tell me in my ear.
Young Pip I think she is very proud.
Miss Havisham Anything else?
Young Pip I think she is very pretty.
Miss Havisham Anything else?

Young Pip I think she is very insulting.
Miss Havisham Anything else?
Young Pip I think I should like to go home.
Miss Havisham What? So soon?
Estella Let him go. I have beggared him.
Miss Havisham Well then, when shall I have you here again? Let me think ...
Young Pip Today is ——
Miss Havisham Tush! I know nothing of days of the week, I know nothing
  of weeks of the year. Come again after six days. Estella, take him down.

Young Pip offers Miss Havisham his hand

  Go, Pip ...

Estella takes Young Pip downstairs

Pip (*to the audience*) My coarse hands and my common boots had never
  troubled me before, but they troubled me now. I determined to ask Joe why
  he had ever taught me to call those picturecards jacks, which ought to be
  called knaves. I wished Joe had been more genteelly brought up; then I
  should have been so, too.
Estella Why don't you cry?
Young Pip Because I don't want to.
Estella You do. You have been crying until you are half-blind, and you are
  near crying again now.

Estella pushes Young Pip out, towards the forge area

The Lights cross-fade from Miss Havisham's house to the forge kitchen

Joe and Mrs Joe are in the kitchen, Joe smoking his pipe and Mrs Joe working

Young Pip comes to the threshold

Mrs Joe Bed!
Pip It is a miserable thing to feel ashamed of home.

The Lights fade as if an episode has ended

SCENE 3

*A Light comes up on Miss Havisham's house, picking out the young Herbert
Pocket. He takes off his jacket, waistcoat and shirt. He splashes himself with
a wet sponge. He goes into a perfect frenzy of shadow-boxing and eccentric
footwork*

Pip (*to the audience*) There was a family named Pocket who were related to Miss Havisham and came on her birthday. Their youngest member was a pale young gentleman.

Young Pip enters on one of his visits

Herbert, still shadow-boxing, confronts Young Pip

Young Pip Good-afternoon.
Herbert I say, who let you in, prowling boy?
Young Pip Miss Estella.

Estella appears on the stairs, watching

Herbert Then come and fight.

Young Pip looks bemusedly at Herbert, who dodges and feints and dances and weaves in front of him. Then Young Pip shoots out his fist, simple and straight, and floors Herbert

Young Pip (*stepping over Herbert*) Good-afternoon.
Herbert (*being stepped over*) Same to you.

SCENE 4

Young Pip is unexpectedly confronted by Estella

Herbert exits

Estella Boy! You may kiss me, if you like. (*She offers Pip her cheek*)

Pip kisses Estella's cheek

There! Am I pretty?
Young Pip Yes, I think you are very pretty.
Estella Am I insulting?
Young Pip Not so much so as you have been.
Estella Not so much so?
Young Pip No.

Estella slaps Young Pip's face, hard

Estella Now? You little coarse monster, what do you think of me now?

Young Pip I shall not tell you.

Estella Then why don't you cry again, you little wretch?

Young Pip Because I'll never cry for you again. (*He moves past Estella to Miss Havisham's room*)

Pip (*to the audience*) Which, I suppose, was as false a declaration as ever was made. I was inwardly crying for her then. I inwardly cry for her now.

SCENE 5

The Lights cross-fade to Miss Havisham's room. Miss Havisham's chair is empty

Young Pip enters Miss Havisham's room

Miss Havisham appears and sits in her chair

Miss Havisham So ... once again the days have worn away, have they?

Pip Yes, ma'am. Today is —

Miss Havisham A day I don't suffer to be spoken of. Today is my birthday. (*She rises*) Walk me. Walk me!

Young Pip Yes, ma'am.

Young Pip supports Miss Havisham. They look out at an unseen room

Miss Havisham Tell me what you see.

Young Pip I see a table.

Miss Havisham It is upon that table I am to be laid out when I am dead. They shall come and look at me here! What do you think that is? There, on the table where the cobwebs are.

Young Pip I can't guess what it is, ma'am.

Miss Havisham It's a great cake, Pip. A bride-cake. Mine! On this day of the year, long before you were born, it was brought here. It and I have worn away together. The mice have gnawed at it, and sharper teeth than teeth of mice have gnawed at me. When the ruin is complete, and when they lay me dead, in my bride's dress on the bride's table, that will be the finished curse upon him. (*She pauses. She seems to have forgotten Young Pip's presence*)

Young Pip If you please, am I to play at cards with Miss Estella?

Miss Havisham I think you are too old for play. And I think you are too young to have a heart a woman may break. A young tree will only bend; did you know that, Pip?

Young Pip (*puzzled*) So they say, ma'am.

Miss Havisham Tell me again the name of that blacksmith of yours.

Estella and Joe enter at the bottom of the stairs. Estella leads Joe up the stairs

Young Pip Joe Gargery, ma'am.
Miss Havisham You had better be apprenticed to him at once. Let him come here, and let him bring your indentures.

Joe and Estella enter Miss Havisham's room. Estella stands behind Miss Havisham's chair

Miss Havisham You are the husband of the sister of this boy?

Joe remains silent

Are you the husband of the sister of this boy?
Joe Which I meantersay, Pip, as I hup and married your sister, and I were at the time what you might call a single man.
Miss Havisham And you have reared the boy with the intention of taking him for your apprentice?
Joe You know, Pip, as you and me were ever friends ——
Young Pip (*in a low voice*) Not to me, Joe ... (*He tries to indicate to Joe that he should address his replies to Miss Havisham and not himself*)

Estella is amused, as much by Young Pip's embarrassment as by Joe's awkwardness

Joe — and it were looked forward as betwixt us as calc'lated to lead to Larks. Wot larks, eh, Pip?
Miss Havisham (*another approach*) Was he to be your apprentice? Does he like the trade?
Joe Which it is well beknown to yourself, Pip, that it were the great wish of your own heart.
Miss Havisham Very well. Have you brought his indentures with you?
Joe Well, Pip, you know you yourself see me put 'em in my 'at, and therefore you know as they are 'ere.

Joe takes the indentures from his hat and gives them to Young Pip, who passes them to Miss Havisham. Estella laughs loudly enough for Young Pip to hear

Miss Havisham You expected no premium with the boy?

Joe is silent

Young Pip Joe, why don't you answer?

Joe (*hurt*) Pip, which I meantersay that were not a question requiring a answer betwixt yourself and me, and which you know the answer to be full well "No". You know it to be "No", Pip, and wherefore should I say it?

Miss Havisham Pip has earned a premium here, and here it is. (*She produces a small bag*) There are five-and-twenty guineas in this bag. Give it to your master, Pip. (*She hands the bag to Young Pip*)

Young Pip Take it, Joe.

Young Pip gives the bag to Joe, who accepts it

Joe This is wery liberal on your part, Pip. And it is as such received and grateful welcome, though never looked for, far nor near nor nowheres.

Estella laughs again, behind her hand

(*Clearing his throat; a speech is to be attempted*) Now, old chap, may we do our duty ——

Young Pip Joe, I think we should ——

Joe — both on us by one and another and by them which your ... (*he flounders*) which your liberal present have ... (*he becomes lost*) conweyed to be ... for the satisfaction of mind of them as never ... and from myself far be it. (*Proudly, he encores*) From myself far be it!

Miss Havisham Goodbye, Pip.

Young Pip Am I to come again, Miss Havisham?

Miss Havisham No. Gargery is your master now and will so remain unless and until providence may otherwise dispose. Go, Pip.

Joe leaves

Young Pip stares at Estella as if expecting a sign. She laughs again, not spontaneously, as before, but meaning to hurt

Mrs Joe and Pumblechook enter the kitchen and wait for Joe

SCENE 6

The Lights cross-fade to the kitchen

Joe enters

Mrs Joe Well? Where is he? Or has Miss Havisham thought to keep him to herself, and good riddance?

Joe Pip, old chap.

Young Pip turns away from Estella and goes into the kitchen area

Mrs Joe There you are. I wonder you condescend to come back to such poor society as this, I am sure I do!

Joe Miss Havisham made it very partick'ler that we should give you ... were it compliments or respects, Pip?

Young Pip Compliments.

Joe Which that were my own belief: her *compliments* to Mrs J. Gargery.

Mrs Joe La de da. Much good they'll do me! And ——

Joe Ehh?

Mrs Joe Was that all she gave?

Joe As to which question meaning was there something giv' that were more than compliments ——

Mrs Joe Gargery!

Joe — and, if such being the case, were it Pip as were the recipipient ——

Mrs Joe What did she give him?

Joe What Miss Havisham give Pip was nothing.

Pumblechook Nothing?

Joe What Miss Havisham giv', she giv' to his friends — I mean, into the hands of his sister Mrs J. Gargery.

Pumblechook Ah-ha! To you, Mum. Listen to this.

Joe What would present company say to ten pounds?

Mrs Joe They'd say pretty well. Not too much, but pretty well.

Joe It's more than that, then.

Pumblechook It's more than that, Mum.

Mrs Joe Why, you don't mean to say ——

Pumblechook Yes, I do, Mum, but wait a bit. Go on, Joseph. Good in you. Go on!

Joe What would present company say to twenty pound?

Mrs Joe Handsome would be the word.

Joe Well, then. It's more than twenty pound.

Pumblechook It's more than twenty pounds, Mum. It's more than twenty pounds. Good again! Follow her up, Joseph!

Joe Then to make an end of it, it's five-and-twenty pound.

Pumblechook shakes hands with Mrs Joe

Pumblechook It's five-and-twenty pound, Mum, and it's no more than your merits. Now you see, Joseph and wife, that I am one who always goes right through with what he has begun.

Mrs Joe Goodness knows, Uncle Pumblechook, we're deeply beholden to
  you.
Pumblechook Never mind me. A pleasure's a pleasure, all the world over.
  Enjoy it, Mum.

*All except Pip troop off. We hear the voices of Joe, Mrs Joe and Pumblechook
offstage, laughing and in celebration, perhaps with a song from Joe*

*Pip stands apart from the others, the cause of the celebration but not part of
it*

Pip (*to the audience*) Thus encouraged, my sister declared that we must have
  a dinner out of the windfall, and so we did, at the *Blue Boar* to which we
  were conveyed in the Pumblechookian chaise, and Mr Wopsle the church
  clerk came, and Mr Hubble the wheelwright came, with Mrs Hubble. And
  such was my sister's merriment that the commercials downstairs sent their
  compliments and to say that it *was* the *Blue Boar* and not the *Tumblers'
  Arms*. And I knew Joe's trade, good as it was, honest as it was, was not for
  me. I had liked it once, but once was not now.

Scene 7

*The Lights cross-fade from the pub to Miss Havisham's room, leaving Pip lit
in isolation*

Pumblechook exits

Joe and Mrs Joe move to the kitchen area and Joe sits down

*Miss Havisham appears in her room, looking down at Young Pip from her
chair. He remains at the lower level*

Miss Havisham How, then? You here again? What do you want?
Young Pip If you please, ma'am, I came to see how you were.
Miss Havisham I live and I do not live. As for you. I hope you want nothing.
  You'll get nothing.
Young Pip No, indeed, Miss Havisham. I only wanted you to know that I
  have been a year at my apprenticeship and am always much obliged to you.
Miss Havisham There, there! Come now and then. Come on your birthday.
  You are looking about you? Is it for Estella?
Young Pip I hope she is well.
Miss Havisham She is very well. She is abroad, educating for a lady; far out
  of reach; prettier than ever; admired by all who see her. (*Maliciously*) Do
  you feel that you have lost her, Pip?

Young Pip I'm sure I never had her, ma'am.
Miss Havisham You have become pert. Be off with you, then.

Miss Havisham exits

The Lights fade on Miss Havisham's room

Pip (*to the audience*) Joe, so Miss Havisham had said, was my master now and would so remain, and until providence should otherwise dispose. Alas, providence did not much frequent our part of the country...

SCENE 8

A Light comes up DS. *Mrs Joe comes forward into it*

Such neglect by providence was more than my unhappy sister could complain of, for in short time she fell ill of a stroke and lay for ever after insensible and between life and death.

Mrs Joe removes her bonnet and shawl. She undoes the string that holds her hair tight and pulled back. She discards a garment and perhaps puts on a brighter apron. She becomes Biddy, younger than Mrs Joe, softer, more gentle

And that was how Biddy came to us to be a nurse to Mrs Joe and all besides to Joe and me. How to describe her? Perhaps it will suffice to say that whatever Mrs Joe had been Biddy was not, and whatever Mrs Joe had not been, Biddy was.

Biddy smiles, and the metamorphosis is complete. Humming to herself, she picks up and tidies away the garments shed by Mrs Joe

The Lights come up in the kitchen. Joe is asleep in his chair

Young Pip sits at the kitchen table and painstakingly copies words out of a book. Biddy looks over his shoulder and makes an amendment, then takes up her sewing. During the following, Pip goes into the kitchen area, removes his coat and hangs it up. He takes down and puts on a blacksmith's leather apron

Pip (*to the audience*) Biddy had been a scholar at an evening school in the village, and, the better to make myself uncommon, I asked her if she would impart all her learning to me. It was a source of wonderment that no matter how hard I toiled, she contrived to stay in front of me like a morning star, that was always beckoning and never to be caught up with ...

Biddy Why, Pip, I suppose I must catch education, like a cough.
Young Pip Biddy ...

Biddy puts down her sewing

    I want —— (*He breaks off, seeing that Pip is now ready to take over*)
Pip — I want to be a gentleman.
Biddy Oh, I wouldn't, if I was you. I don't think it would answer.

*Pip moves into the kitchen and takes Young Pip's place. Young Pip takes up
Pip's previous position, so that Young Pip is now the observer*

Pip I am disgusted with my calling and my life. I have never taken to either
    since I was bound. So don't be absurd.
Biddy Am I absurd? I'm sure I don't mean to be.
Pip If only I could have been but half as fond of the forge as when I was little
    — why, you and Joe would have wanted nothing. And Joe and I could have
    gone partners when I was out of my time. And I might even have grown
    up to keep company with you. We might have walked out of a Sunday. I
    should have been good enough for *you*, shouldn't I, Biddy?
Biddy Yes, I am not over-particular.
Pip Instead, see how I am going on. I could have been coarse and common
    and none the worse for it if nobody had told me so.
Biddy It was neither a very true nor a very polite thing to say. Who said it?
Pip The beautiful young lady at Miss Havisham's. I desire to be a gentleman
    on her account.
Biddy To spite her? Or to gain her over? Which is it, Pip?
Young Pip (*in anguish*) *I* don't know!
Pip (*more composed*) I don't know.
Biddy You know, you might the better spite her by caring nothing for her
    words. As for the other, I should think she is not worth gaining over.
Pip I admire her dreadfully.
Biddy Poor Pip. This is one lesson I can't bid you learn by heart.
Pip No. At least, I can always come to you with my troubles.
Biddy Until you're a gentleman.
Pip You know I shall never be, so that's always. I wish you could put me
    right. If only I could get myself to fall in love with you, *that* would be the
    thing for me.
Biddy But you never will, you see.
Jaggers (*bellowing; off*) Joseph Gargery!
Biddy Who on earth is that?
Young Pip Prov-id-ence!

Young Pip exits

Jaggers appears

Jaggers I seek the blacksmith, by name Gargery.

Biddy admits Jaggers. Joe wakes up

Joseph Gargery?
Joe Here is the man.
Jaggers You have an apprentice, commonly known as Pip?
Pip And I am here!

Jaggers thrusts his hat at Biddy. He looks for a moment at Joe and Pip and bites the side of his finger: a mannerism

Jaggers My name is Jaggers and I am a lawyer in London. I have unusual business to transact with you, and it is not of my originating. What I have to do, I do as the confidential agent of another. No less, no more, Joseph Gargery. I am the bearer of an offer to relieve you of this young fellow, your apprentice. You would not object to cancel his indentures for his own good?
Joe Lord forbid that I should want anything for not standing in Pip's way.
Jaggers Lord forbidding is pious, but not to the purpose. The question is, would you want anything?
Joe (*disliking Jaggers*) The answer is "No".
Jaggers Very well. Recollect the admission you have made and don't try to go from it presently.
Joe Who's a-going to try?
Jaggers I don't say anybody is. Do you keep a dog?
Joe Yes, I keep a dog.
Jaggers Bear in mind then that Brag is a good dog, but Holdfast is a better. Now I turn to this young fellow. And the communication I have got to make is that he has great expectations.
Biddy (*with a gasp*) Oh. (*She turns to leave*)

Young Pip puts a hand on Biddy's arm

Biddy exits nonetheless

Jaggers Now, Master Pip, you are to understand, first, that you shall always bear the name of Pip. You will have no objection, I dare say, to your great expectations being encumbered with that easy condition?

Pip (*breathlessly*) I have no objection.

Jaggers I should think not! You are to understand, secondly, that the name of the person who is your benefactor shall remain a profound secret until that person chooses to reveal it. It is the intention of the person to reveal it at first hand by word of mouth to yourself, but when or where that intention may be carried out, I cannot say. It may be years hence. Meanwhile, if you have a suspicion in your own breast, keep it in your own breast. Again, not a very difficult condition with which to encumber such a rise in fortune, but if you have any objection, now is the time to mention it.

Pip Again, I have no objection.

Jaggers Again, I should think not. Henceforth, you will please consider me your guardian. When will you come to London?

Pip *London?*

Jaggers Let us say this day week. You should have some new clothes and they should not be working clothes. Shall I leave you twenty guineas? (*He counts out the money from a long purse*) Well, Joseph Gargery, you look dumbfounded.

Joe I am!

Jaggers Give voice, nonetheless. What if I were empowered to make you a present as a compensation ...

Joe (*bridling*) Hey?

Jaggers A sum of money for the loss of his services?

Joe Money? Do you think money can make compensation to me?...for the loss of the little child that come to the forge, and ever the best of friends?

Pip We shall always be friends, Joe — always.

Jaggers Now, Joseph Gargery, I warn you this is your last chance. If you mean to take a present that I have in my charge to make you, speak out. If, on the contrary ——

Joe advances on Jaggers, threateningly, during the following. Jaggers backs away in alarm

Joe Which I meantersay, that if you come into my place bull-baiting and badgering me, come out! Which I meantersay as sech, if you're a man, come on! Which I meantersay that what I say, I meantersay and stand or fall by!

Biddy comes in

Jaggers Well, Pip, I think the sooner you leave here — as you are to be a gentleman — the better.

Biddy To be a gentleman?

Jaggers You shall receive my printed address. You can take a hackney-coach at the stage-coach office in London and come straight to me. As for you, Joseph Gargery ——

Joe growls and seems as if about to resume his attack

—— I bid you good-day.

Jaggers exits

Pip removes the leather apron so that he is the "London" Pip again

Biddy Pip, what has happened?
Joe Pip's a gentleman of fortun' then, and God bless him in it.

Biddy gasps. It is a sigh as if this is something she had both expected and yet feared

The Lights come up in the Satis House area. Pip moves into this area

Biddy Mr Gargery, if I forget my place, I ask pardon, but is this what you wish for him?
Joe Why, with much of my heart. Which I meantersay, dear Biddy, that never having seen a gentleman, what I wish, I wish from ignorance.

Joe and Biddy exit

SCENE 9

Pip Miss Havisham!

Miss Havisham appears

Miss Havisham You? Well, Pip!
Pip I start for London tomorrow, Miss Havisham, and I thought you would kindly not mind my taking leave of you.
Miss Havisham This is a gay figure, Pip.
Pip I have come into such good fortune since I saw you last, Miss Havisham. And I am so grateful for it.
Miss Havisham I have seen Mr Jaggers. I have heard about it, Pip. And you are adopted by a rich person?
Pip Yes, Miss Havisham.

Miss Havisham Not named?
Pip Not named.
Miss Havisham Well, you have a promising career before you. Be good.
   Deserve it and abide by Mr Jaggers' ins—— (*As in "instructions"*)

Pip, in an excess of gratitude, drops on one knee and kisses Miss Havisham's
hand, causing her to break off

There, there! You will always keep the name of Pip, you know.
Pip Yes, Miss Havisham.
Miss Havisham Then goodbye, Pip. And remember your benefactor.

The Light on Miss Havisham goes out

Pip goes into the kitchen area

Scene 10

Biddy Is it time, Pip? Let me call Joe from the forge. You mustn't get soot
   and ashes on your fine clothes.
Pip Biddy, I should be glad of a private word. I have a favour to ask. It is that
   you will always take the opportunity to help Joe on a little.
Biddy How help him on?
Pip Well, Joe is the dearest fellow who ever lived, but in some way he is
   rather backward. I mean in his learning and his manners.
Biddy Oh, his manners. Won't his manners do, then?
Pip Hear me out. I mean it for his good. One day it may be that I can remove
   Joe into a higher place in the world. His manners would hardly do him
   justice.
Biddy Don't you think he knows that?
Pip Well, perhaps.
Biddy No, not perhaps, Pip. Rather say most certainly. Have you never
   considered that he may be proud?
Pip (*with disdain*) Joe? Proud?
Biddy Oh, there are many kinds of pride. Pride is not all of one kind. Joe may
   be too proud to let anyone take him out of a place that he fills well and with
   respect. He may be backward in learning, but he knows where his place is.
Pip Biddy, I did not expect to see this in you. You are envious, and grudging.
Biddy If you have the heart to think so, then yes, say so. If you have the heart
   to think so.
Pip It's a — bad side of human nature.
Biddy So it is, if it were true. But I thought a gentleman was never unjust.

Joe comes in with Pumblechook, who is carrying a small basket

Joe See, Pip, old chap … look who has come to drive you to the coach.
Pumblechook My dear friend, my young protégé ... I give you joy. And to think that I should have been the humble instrument leading up to this. What a proud reward.
Pip If you please, a certain name is neither to be uttered nor hinted at.
Pumblechook Of course, not one word, God bless her! Now here for your journey is a chicken had round from the *Boar*, here is a tongue had round from the *Boar,* here's one or two little things had round from the *Boar*, which you may not despise. But do I see before me him as I sported with in his times of happy infancy? And may I? *May* I? (*He extends a hand*)

Pip shakes Pumblechook's hand

Pip Well, it's time to go.
Biddy Goodbye, Pip.

She makes an attempt to be distant with him, but her good nature overcomes her, and they embrace lovingly

Pip Goodbye, Biddy. Take care of him.
Biddy Yes!
Pip Joe ...
Joe Well, Pip ...
Pumblechook (*intruding*) Call it a weakness, if you will, but may I?*May* I?

Again, Pumblechook shakes hands with Pip. He stifles a tear

Pumblechook rushes out

Joe Ever the best of friends, Pip, dear old Pip. Which, I meantersay, why, in no time you'll come back to us same as ever was, and then ... oh, Pip, wot larks!
Pip (*to the audience*) To my shame, it was easier to go from them than I had supposed. The morning mist lifted. A curtain had risen. I was on my way to London! And instead of our humble village church I saw a great dome, white in the sun. A single smoking chimney-pot became ten thousand. Instead of cottages I saw palaces; instead of a lone farmer's boy, I saw multitudes. And instead of dear Joe toiling at his forge, I saw a man sitting on top of the highest chair in all the world.

ACT III
London

SCENE 1

Pip picks up a portmanteau and sets off for London. Young Pip follows with his belongings in a brown paper parcel

The Lights cross-fade from Joe and Biddy to Wemmick sitting on an impossibly high stool: he is "a dry man, short in stature, whose expression seems to have been chipped out with a dull-edged chisel". Pip, carrying his portmanteau, enters Wemmick's area

Wemmick Mr Jaggers is in court at present. Am I addressing Mr Pip?
Pip Yes, sir.
Wemmick You mustn't "sir" me, you know. I'm Mr Jaggers' clerk. Will you be pleased to wait? His time being money, he won't be longer than he can help.

Pip sits

Never been in London before?
Pip No, si ... No.
Wemmick *I* was new here once. Rum to think of it now. Now I know the moves of it.
Pip Is it a very wicked place?
Wemmick You may get cheated, robbed or murdered in London. But there are people everywhere to do that for you.
Jaggers *(off)* It's Newgate for you, you sanctimonious rogue, and serve you right if they hang you. Now get out of my way!
Wemmick Ah, that's him. He's just finishing with our client.

Jaggers comes in wearing his court dress. He flings his brief at Wemmick

Mr Pip is here.
Jaggers Ah. No need to ask if you had a comfortable journey. You did not, for no-one ever does, and there's an end to it. Is the name of Mr Matthew Pocket familiar to you?
Pip Pocket? No, I ... ah ...
Jaggers He lives out in the country, at Hammersmith, five miles west of here. He is to be your tutor.

Pip opens his mouth to speak

And no, you are not to live there. Wemmick will take you to the rooms of your tutor's son, Mr Pocket Junior, where a bed has been sent in for your accommodation. Wemmick will give you a list of tradesmen and pay you your allowance quarterly. It is a liberal sum; however, I shall pull you up if I find you trying to outrun the constable. Of course you will go wrong, but that's no fault of mine. Good day. Wemmick, in the case of Spooney — when you return see if you can find me a witness who's a plausible rogue instead of a blundering booby.

Jaggers exits

SCENE 2

Wemmick climbs down from his high stool. He and Pip mime walking through the streets of London. London noises and street cries fade in

Pip Do you live in these parts, Mr Wemmick?

Wemmick No, I live across the river in Walworth, by the Elephant and Castle. Some day, if you are so disposed, you must come and visit. You don't object to an Aged Parent, I hope?

Pip Not at all.

Wemmick My parent, that is The Aged P., not going out much, is fond of visitors. Ah! And unless I'm mistaken, here comes the mountain, surely on its way to meet Mahomet.

Herbert Pocket appears, carrying fruit in a paper bag

Mr Pocket, there you are. This is Mr Pip.

Herbert Mr Pip!

Pip Mr Pocket!

Herbert How do you do. We meet by accident. The fact is, I thought, coming from the country, you might like a little fruit after dinner, so I went to Covent Garden to get it good.

Wemmick Mr Pip, I'll leave you in the proper hands. As I keep the cash, we shall most likely meet pretty often. Good-day.

Pip (*offering his hand*) Good-day.

Wemmick Oh ... you're in the habit of shaking hands, are you? Very glad, I'm sure, to make your acquaintance.

Wemmick goes off

Pip and Herbert face each other. There is a moment of silence, then Pip extends his hand. Herbert, overloaded, manages to respond in kind; then:

Herbert Lord bless me!
Pip Yes?
Herbert You're the prowling boy!
Pip And you are the pale young gentleman!
Herbert The idea of its being you!
Pip The idea of its being you!
Herbert Well, I hope you'll be magnanimous enough to forgive me for
knocking you senseless!

*Pip blinks at this, but they both laugh, shake hands and go directly into their
lodgings*

The Lights cross-fade to Pip's and Herbert's lodgings

SCENE 3

*Herbert moves a table into place and sets it for dinner with plates, a tureen
and cutlery*

Herbert Mr Pip, do you know why I was in that garden? Because Miss
Havisham had sent for me, as she sent for you.
Pip Indeed?
Herbert Alas, she didn't take a fancy to me. If she had done, I might have
been what-do-you-called-it to Estella. Affianced. Engaged. Betrothed.
What's-his-named.
Pip How did you ever bear the disappointment?
Herbert Easily. She's a tartar.
Pip Miss Havisham?
Herbert I don't say no to that, but I meant Estella. That girl is hard and
haughty and capricious and has been brought up to wreak revenge on all
the male sex.
Pip I beg to disagree.
Herbert Of course she is also charming, warm-hearted and lovable.
Pip May I ask what relation is she to Miss Havisham?
Herbert None. Only adopted. Poor thing.
Pip But why should Miss Havisham wish to wreak revenge on all the male
sex?
Herbert My dear fellow, don't you know? I thought Mr Jaggers might have
been in a story-telling mood.
Pip (*with incredulity*) Mr Jaggers?
Herbert No, perhaps not. He is Miss Havisham's man of business, you
know. (*He invites Pip to sit at the table*) Shall we?

Pip sits. Herbert does likewise and mimes the pouring of wine and the serving of food. They mime eating the first course which is taken with a spoon. Pip uses his spoon overhand

Pip Herbert, you know that I was brought up a blacksmith in that country place and am foreign to the ways of politeness. I would take it as a kindness if you would give me a hint, whenever I go wrong.

Herbert My dear fellow, with the greatest pleasure. Now, concerning Miss Havisham. She was a spoilt child. Her father was very rich and very proud. He was a brewer. A gentleman may keep a brewery, you know, but not a public house, even if a public house may keep a gentleman. And let me break off to say that in London the spoon is not generally used overhand, but under.

Pip I beg your pardon.

Herbert Not at all. It has two advantages. You get at your mouth better, and you save a good deal of the attitude of opening oysters.

During the following they eat with knives and forks; in doing so, Pip puts his knife in his mouth and his fork far too far into it

So Miss Havisham was an heiress and looked after as a great match. There appeared a certain man. Named Compeyson. Mark that well lest you thoughtlessly give utterance to the name in Miss Havisham's hearing.

Pip On my soul Herbert I should be less inclined to give utterance to the word, if I had never heard it.

Herbert True. I beg your pardon.

Pip Not at all. I beg your pardon.

Herbert Compeyson was not, in spite of his affectations, a gentleman — no amount of varnish can ever hide the grain of the wood — but he pursued Miss Havisham, and she idolized him. Well, to make a beginning and an end to him — breaking off merely to say that it is not the custom to put the knife into the mouth, and the fork no further in than necessary. (*He resumes*) A wedding was fixed, the wedding tour planned, the guests invited. The day came, but not the bridegroom. Compeyson wrote a letter, heartlessly breaking the marriage off, and she has since never looked upon the light of day.

Pip And Estella? You say she was adopted. When adopted?

Herbert Ever since I have heard of a Miss Havisham, I have heard of an Estella. I know no more.

Pip And what of you? Herbert, is it impolite to ask are you a gentleman?

Herbert Good heavens, no. I am a capitalist. I work in a counting-house and look about me. I am paid not a penny, but the grand thing is, to look about

you. You see your opening, you swoop upon it, and there you — um —are!
Simple.
Pip I see. *I* am to become a gentleman.
Herbert How very agreeable.
Pip It isn't, at all. I'm sure it's far beyond me.
Herbert Nonsense. You have a brain and most gentlemen have none. You
will have gone far past me in a week and be a stranger to your own self in
a six-month. My dear fellow, to your future. (*He raises a glass*)

*Pip rises, puts on a floral dressing-gown and takes a note from his pocket .
He reads it*

Scene 4

*The Lights come up in the forge area. Biddy and Joe are there. Biddy is
finishing writing the same note that Pip is reading. Biddy reads the letter
aloud and Joe listens*

Biddy "My dear Mr Pip, I write this by request of Mr Gargery, for to let you
know that he is going to London and would be glad, if agreeable, to be
allowed to see you. He will call on Tuesday morning at nine o'clock. It is
six months now. Your poor sister is much the same as when you left. We
talk of you in the kitchen every night and wonder what you are saying and
doing. If now considered in the light of a liberty, excuse it for the love of
poor old days. No more, dear Mr Pip, from Your ever obliged and
affectionate servant, Biddy."

Joe takes down his hat and puts it on

Joe What larks!
Biddy "PS. He wishes me most particular to write *What larks*. He says you
will understand. I hope and do not doubt it will be agreeable to see him,
even though a gentleman, for you had ever a good heart, and he is a worthy,
worthy man."
Joe What larks!
Biddy "He wishes me most particular to write again ... "
Pip "What larks!"

Pip crumples the letter, not pleased to receive it

The Lights cross-fade from the forge area to the London area

Biddy remains in the forge area

SCENE 5

Joe moves across the stage to Pip's and Herbert's lodgings, where tea things are set up. Pip goes to admit his visitor

Pip Joe! Dear Joe!

Joe wipes his feet and keeps on wiping them

  How are you, Joe?
Joe How air you, Pip?

Joe takes Pip's hands and works them up and down, pump-like

Pip I am glad to see you, Joe. Give me your hat.
Joe (*holding on to his hat with both hands*) Which you have growed, and that swelled and that gentle-folked, as to be sure you are a honour to your king and country.
Pip And you, Joe, look wonderfully well.
Joe Thank God, I'm ekerval to most. And Biddy, she's ever right and ready. And all friends is no backerder, if no forarder.

  Herbert appears and comes forward

Pip Oh — Herbert. May I introduce Mr Gargery. Joe, this is my friend, Mr Pocket.
Herbert (*warmly*) Oh, how very pleased I am. How do you do?
Joe (*giving his hat to Herbert*) Your servant, sir. Which I hope as you two gentlemen get your 'ealths in this close spot. For the present may be a werry good inn, according to London opinions, but I wouldn't keep a pig in it myself, not in the case that I wished him to fatten wholesome and to eat with a meller flavour to him.
Herbert Won't you sit down, Mr Gargery!

Joe does so. Herbert gives Joe's hat to Pip. Joe takes it back

  Do you take tea or coffee?
Joe Thankee, sir. (*The hat flies out of his hands*)

Herbert catches the hat

  I'll take whichever is most agreeable to yourself.
Herbert Then shall we have coffee?

Joe Thankee, sir, since you *are* so kind to make choice of coffee, I will not
run contrairy to your opinions. But don't you never find it a little 'eating?
Herbert Say tea, then. (*He pours tea*) When did you come to town, Mr
Gargery?
Joe Were it yesterday? No, it were not. Yes, it were. Yes.

Pip sits, silent and mortified

Herbert And have you seen anything of London yet?
Joe Why, yes, sir. I been to look at the Blacking Warehouse. But it didn't
come up to its likeness in the red bills at the shop doors, which I meantersay
as it is there drawed too architectooralooral.
Herbert I say. Is that the time? I must be off to the City to — er, look about
me. Mr Gargery, forgive me. It has been the most *singular* pleasure. (*To
Pip*) Until this evening.

   Herbert exits

A moment's silence. Joe gets awkwardly to his feet

Joe Us two being now alone, sir ——
Pip Joe, how can you call me "sir"?
Joe Us two being now alone I will now conclude — leastways begin — to
mention what have led to my having had the present honour. For was it not
that my only wish were to be useful to you, I should not have had the honour
of breaking wittles in the company and abode of gentlemen.
Pip Do sit down, Joe.
Joe Well, sir, this is how it were, it being as such as Miss 'Avisham sent word
by Pumblechook, saying as that she wished to speak to me.
Pip Miss Havisham?
Joe So having cleaned myself, I go and I see Miss A.
Pip Miss A?
Joe Which I say, sir, Miss A, or otherwise 'Avisham. Her expression air then
as follering: "If you air in correspondence with Mr Pip, would you tell him
that which Estella has come home and will be calling on him in London as
how she has need of a service."
Pip Estella? Coming here?
Joe Biddy, when I got home and asked her fur to write to you, Biddy says:
"I know he will be very glad to have it by word of mouth, it is holiday-time,
you want to see him, go!" (*He rises*) I have now concluded, sir, and, Pip?
I wish you ever well and ever prospering to a greater and a greater height.
Pip But you are not going now, Joe?
Joe Yes, I am.

Pip But you are coming back to dinner?

Joe No, I am not. Pip, dear old chap, if there's been any fault today, it's mine. You and me is not two figures to be together in London, nor anywheres else but what is private and beknown. It ain't that I'm proud, but I want to be right. I'm wrong out of the forge, the kitchen or off th' meshes. You won't find half so much fault in me if you come and put your head in at the forge window and see Joe the blacksmith there, at the old anvil, in the burnt apron, sticking to the old 'ammering work. I'm dull but I hope I've beat out something nigh the rights of this.

Pip Joe...

Joe God bless you, dear old Pip, old chap.

Joe moves to the kitchen area. Pip looks after him, dismayed, angry with himself

The Lights cross-fade to the kitchen area

Joe and Pip sit. Biddy moves to the kitchen area and reaches to comfort Joe

Pip leaves his room and exits

Joe is not to be comforted. He gets up and exits simultaneously

END OF PART I

PART II

ACT IV
Carriage to Coach

SCENE 1

We have reached the point in time at which the play started

A small seat has been placed DC; Pip and the grown-up Estella sit on it. The seat will represent a moving carriage taking Pip and Estella to Richmond. Young Pip (as yet unrecognizable, and with a post horn) is the driver

The Lights come up C. There is the sound of other traffic: carriage wheels, hooves, the jangle of harness

Pip Driver, not by Hammersmith. Take us the other way, by Kew.

Estella That is not our road, Pip ...

Pip I thought we might make a stop by the river. We shall be at Richmond soon enough.

Estella Driver, the gentleman was mistaken. Go the direct way. Pip, will you never take warning?

Pip Of what?

Estella If you don't know, you are blind. Will you take warning of me?

Pip Never.

Estella (*shaking her head*) Very well, then. Let me go round about. Do you know a man named Drummle?

Pip I know a Bentley Drummle.

Estella Ah? Is he a friend of yours?

Pip Not he. He is a blotchy, sprawly, sulky fellow. He lodged for a time with my tutor who, as far as Drummle was concerned, had a separate calling as a grinder.

Estella A what?

Pip It is a name given to a teacher who takes backward pupils. He grinds dull blades.

Estella Is Bentley Drummle a dull blade, then?

Pip Whenever he takes up a book, he does so as if the writer had done him an injury. Are you in some way interested in the fellow?

Estella No, but the fellow seems to be interested in me.

Pip What? The devil, you say! I beg your pardon.

Estella says nothing

Estella, you would surely not in any way encourage him?

Estella Moths and all kinds of ugly creatures hover about a lighted candle. Can the candle help it?

Pip I think the Estella can help it.

Estella (*laughing*) Perhaps she can.

Pip You know Drummle is despised.

Estella Well?

Pip He is a deficient, ill-tempered, lowering fellow with nothing to recommend him but money.

Estella (*again*) Well?

Pip (*to the driver*) Stop. Stop here. (*To Estella*) If I am to talk to you of these matters, it must be face to face. (*He alights and holds out his hand to help Estella down*) Please?

Estella (*alighting*) Well, Pip, you have stopped by the river after all.

Pip Estella, I implore you. You cannot throw away your graces and attractions on a boor, the lowest in the crowd.

Estella Can't I? Perhaps you would rather I deceived and entrapped *you*?

Pip Then would you deceive and entrap him?

Estella Of course. Him and many others. All of them but you. I mention Drummle because to entice him and his like is what I was bred for.

Pip You would not give your heart to such a creature?

Estella I have no heart. Oh, I have a heart to be stabbed in or shot in, and if it ceased to be I should cease to be. But I there is no place for softness there, or sympathy, or sentiment, or nonsense.

Pip Herbert says ——

Estella Herbert Pocket?

Pip He says that you are to be Miss Havisham's revenge on the male sex.

Estella You already know that, do you? How vexatious. I might have saved my breath instead of spoiling a summer's day.

Pip Of course it is not true.

Estella No?

Pip I'll allow that Miss Havisham may not be as other women. But to sacrifice you — you, Estella! — to a base craving for revenge ... No, I'll not believe it. I will not believe that within the one person, such cruelty and such kindness can both exist ...

Estella Kindness? Miss Havisham? Kindness, you say? (*With sudden ferocity*) Pray tell me, when was that woman ever kind?

Pip She ... Estella, all I possess, all I am, I owe to —— (*He breaks off. He cannot reveal his conviction that Miss Havisham is his benefactor*)

Estella You owe to?

Pip To Providence.

Herbert appears, holding a letter

Herbert (*calling*) Handel — I say!
Estella Richmond, driver!

SCENE 2

Young Pip is revealed as the driver and takes over the role of narrator

Young Pip (*to the audience*) There had come a letter from Biddy.
Pip (*to the audience*) My unhappy sister, having lain close to death these
years past, had taken that final step.
Young Pip (*to the audience*) Naturally, it was no less than my duty to be at
Joe's side at such a time and to do honour to her who had brought me up
by hand.

Joe appears. He wears a hat with mourner's crape on it, but hanging loose

Pip Dear Joe, how are you?
Joe Pip, old chap, you knowed her when she was a fine figure of a ...(*He
becomes emotional*)
Pip Yes, Joe, I did. There, now.
Joe Which I meantersay, I don't deny as what there was times when your
sister come the Mo-gul over us, and that she did throw us back-falls and
drop down upon us heavy when she was on the Ram-page. But we has to
remember, Pip, as how there is much allowed to them as is ——
Pip Given to government, Joe?
Joe — as is master-minds, Pip. Master-minds.
Pip Joe, Biddy's letter did not give particulars of how my sister died.
Joe Why, she said "Joe". All of a sudden, she said "Joe", as plain as you like
and out loud. And she made signs that she wanted me to sit close and for
me to put her arms around my neck. Which as you full well know that
warn't like her, Pip. And so she presently said "Joe" again, and once
"Pardon", and once "Pip". And she never lifted her head up no more.

*After a moment, Pumblechook appears with Biddy. His hat is swathed in
masses of black crape*

Pumblechook (*making for Pip, his hand extended*) Oh, Joseph. Joseph. (*He
sees Pip*) Oh, may I, my dear sir, may I? This is most condescending. What
an honour you do to both them what is living and them what is not. Joseph,

come; it is time to take your place. Oh, but what do I see? Your hat is not funereal. Joseph, this is too bad of you.

Pumblechook sets Joe's hat to rights. Pip and Biddy stand apart from the others

Pip Well, Biddy, this is a sad business. I suppose it will be difficult for you to remain here now?
Biddy Impossible, Mr Pip.
Pip If you are in need of money ——
Biddy I thought I would try to get the place of mistress in the new school nearly finished here. I hope I can teach myself while I teach others.
Pip You did so once before. You shall again. And you will be glad to know that I shall be down here often now. I am not going to leave poor Joe alone.

Biddy does not reply

Biddy, don't you hear me?
Biddy Yes, Mr Pip.
Pip Mr Pip? Biddy, why do you call me by that name? It appears to me to be in bad taste.
Biddy Are you quite sure that you *will* come to see him often?
Pip Biddy!
Biddy And if you do so, will you lodge at the *Blue Boar* then, as you do today? Is that in good taste?
Pip I stay in the village only because because I have a mind to visit Miss Havisham. And I had no wish to come here and perhaps be an inconvenience.
Biddy What? In your own home? An inconvenience?
Pumblechook (*turning to Pip and Biddy*) There, now, we may proceed.
Pip I was saying to Biddy, Joe, that I shall be down soon, and often.
Joe Never too soon, Pip, and never too often, sir.
Pumblechook Pocket-handker-chiefs out! Pocket-handker-chiefs out, all!

SCENE 3

Pip looks towards Biddy as if he had vindicated himself. Instead, he is confronted by the knowing, unwavering stare of Young Pip

Joe emits a great sob and shuffles out

Villagers arrive bearing umbrellas

Biddy You are angry.

Pip No. I am hurt.
Biddy Then don't be. Only let me be hurt, if I am ungenerous.
Pumblechook We are ready. We may proceed.
Young Pip (*to the audience*) And so we went into the churchyard, close to
the parents I never knew: Philip Pirrip, late of this parish, also Georgiana,
wife of the above. And there my sister was laid quietly in the earth while
the larks sang high above it.

SCENE 4

The Lights cross-fade to Miss Havisham's area

Pip moves into Miss Havisham's area

Miss Havisham enters and sits

Miss Havisham Now, then! You here, Pip? When Estella is in London?
Pip My sister has died, Miss Havisham.
Miss Havisham Is she? What of it? The world's a grave. Tell me about
Estella. You have seen her?
Pip Yes.
Miss Havisham And is she beautiful, graceful, well-grown? Do you admire
her?
Pip Everyone must, Miss Havisham.
Miss Havisham Come here.

Pip moves to Miss Havisham. She pulls his head close to hers

Love her, love her, love her! If she favours you, love her. If she wounds you
love her. If she tears your heart to pieces — and as it grows older and
stronger, it will tear more deeply — love her. Say you will.
Pip I always have done. I always shall.
Miss Havisham No. It will come, but not yet. You still love in the way of
a boy. Shall I tell you what love is? It is blind devotion, self-humiliation,
utter submission, trust and belief against yourself and against the world,
giving up your heart to the one who betrays and tears it. As I did! As ——
(*She rears up from her chair, flailing*)

Pip catches Miss Havisham and saves her from falling

(*With sudden awareness*) Pip...
Pip Yes, Miss Havisham?
Miss Havisham That scent. He is here. In this house.
Pip There is no-one here.

Miss Havisham Are you insensible? He is in this room.
Pip You are mistaken truly. There is —— (*He breaks off and looks around*)

Jaggers enters into the light, rolling a silk handkerchief between his fingers. He inhales its scent

Miss Havisham You are as punctual as ever.
Jaggers I am as punctual as ever. And so you are here, Pip? I am glad to see you.
Miss Havisham Jaggers, what mischief are you up to?
Jaggers Mischief? From a man of law? Dear lady, you mistake yourself. Tomorrow is your birthday, Pip.
Pip Is it? I had forgotten.
Jaggers I had not. Tomorrow you come of age. We shall have business to transact, you and I.
Miss Havisham Jaggers, will you leave my Pip alone?
Jaggers Most willingly! If you can bid tomorrow never to come, and if tomorrow does as it is told. (*To Pip*) When do you return to town?
Pip I thought I might ——
Jaggers Good. I have engaged a carriage that will convey us to Rochester. Will you be pleased to be here at seven in the morning?
Miss Havisham Jaggers, I tell you, leave him alone. Your business is here with me.
Jaggers That will detain neither of us.
Miss Havisham The man is a boor!
Jaggers (*ignoring Miss Havisham*) From Rochester we shall take the morning coach — the new express service. I emulate the Spartans, Pip. I deprecate any over-indulgence in creature comforts, but I find myself unable to despise whatever goes quickly.

Scene 5

There is the sound of a post horn. The Lights cross-fade to the seat DS

The people of the play — Joe, Biddy, Wemmick and the others — leap on to the seat as stagecoach passengers. They wear mufflers over their mouths. They form an ungainly mass: precarious, ill-balanced yet balancing, writhing, piled high and utterly at odds with Jaggers' "creature comforts"

Jaggers hustles Pip out of Miss Havisham's room, and they take their places on the seat. Young Pip sounds the post-horn. There is the whinnying of horses

Young Pip To coach! To coach! All passengers for Cross Keys, Wood Street, Cheapside and Charing Cross! All passengers to coach!

Another blast of the post horn signals the "off". The coach starts off, the passengers swaying wildly

Jaggers (*with his handkerchief to his face*) Progress, progress! Where will it all end?

Pip Mr Jaggers, sir ...

Jaggers Hey?

Pip Pray, sir, may I ask you a question?

Jaggers You may, and I may decline to answer it. Put your question.

Pip I thought, begging your pardon, sir, that Miss Havisham seemed afraid of you.

Jaggers That is not a question, Pip, but it invites an observation. Yes, Miss Havisham is afraid of me. It is a condition peculiar to those who fear they may be found out.

Pip Found out? Do you mean, Miss Havisham has a secret, then?

Jaggers She does. She has that much in common, if nothing else, with the entire population of this planet.

Pip Yourself included, sir?

Jaggers I am paid to have secrets, Pip.

Pip Estella's name, Mr Jaggers. Is it Havisham or ——

Jaggers That is another question. (*He pauses*) Is it Havisham or is it what?

Pip Is it Havisham?

Jaggers It is Havisham.

Another post horn is heard, this one more from the distant terminus, announcing the arrival

The passengers alight and hurry off in various directions

Ah, the metropolis! (*He looks at his watch*) Four hours, five and thirty minutes. Mark me, no good will come of it. (*He rises*) Well, Pip ... but no, from today I must call you Mr Pip. Congratulations, *Mr* Pip.

Pip Thank you, sir.

Jaggers If you will come to Gerrard Street this evening, I'll endeavour to give you a dinner worthy of the occasion. And, if he be so disposed, I shall be glad to see your friend, young Mr Pocket. (*He goes towards the "London area" and calls off*) Molly, will you bring in the port! Must my guests expire of sobriety?

ACT V
Jaggers

Scene 1

The Lights cross-fade to the London area

Herbert enters, joins Pip and Jaggers and they all enter the area of Jaggers'
house

During the following, Molly, the maid, enters and serves the port

Jaggers Gentlemen, forgive me. Mr Pocket, I believe you had the floor.
Herbert I merely said that while Handel ——

Jaggers raises an eyebrow

— *that* while Mr Pip, as you call him, is the most proficient of oarsmen, I
dare not go on the river. For one thing, dearest Clara ——
Jaggers Clara?
Pip — Herbert's young lady ——
Jaggers ⎫
Pip ⎬ (*raising their glasses; together*) Clara!
Herbert ⎭
Herbert An angel, sir. Clara is convinced I shall drown. And besides, when
it comes to rowing, I simply do not have the wrists. I mean, compare mine
with Mr Pip's. Handel, roll up your cuffs. Show Mr Jaggers.

Pip shows Jaggers his wrists

There — you see, sir? Mine are twigs, while his are like young oaks. The
village smithy, eh, Handel?
Jaggers If you talk of strength, gentlemen — let me give you a sight of this!

Jaggers catches hold of Molly

Molly, show them your wrist.
Molly Master...please.
Jaggers Let them see both your wrists. Show them. Come.

Molly shows her wrists very reluctantly. They are badly scarred and
disfigured. Jaggers, holding Molly's arm, traces the sinews with his forefinger

There's strength here, young sirs. Very few men have the power of wrist that this woman has. It is remarkable what mere force of grip there is in these. I have had occasion to notice many hands, but I never saw stronger in that respect, in man or woman, than those.

Herbert (*embarrassed*) Remarkable.

Jaggers As you say. That'll do, Molly. You have been admired and can go.

Molly leaves

Well, Pip?

Pip She is like a wild beast tamed.

Jaggers That is what she is.

Herbert Mr Jaggers, how came she by those scars?

Jaggers Sir, that is not a subject to be discussed, even between gentlemen and over a glass of port. Mr Pip, I wish you good health.

Herbert Hear, hear!

Pip Thank you.

They drink

Mr Jaggers, forgive me, but I have wondered if on this occasion ——

Jaggers Now be careful, Pip.

Pip I keep no secrets from Herbert. I have wondered if I am to be told the name of my benefactor.

Jaggers No. Do you have another question?

Pip Is that confidence to be imparted to me soon?

Jaggers Now here we must revert to the evening when we first encountered one another in your village. What did I tell you then, Pip?

Pip You told me it might be years hence when that person appeared.

Jaggers Just so. That's my answer.

Pip Do you suppose it will still be years hence, Mr Jaggers?

Jaggers That's a question I must not be asked. Come now. Ask me instead if on this day you have anything to receive?

Pip Well have I anything to receive, sir?

Jaggers Ah! I thought we should come to that! Mr Pocket is still in your confidence, is he?

Pip Of course. (*He toasts Herbert*) Mr Pocket!

Herbert Mr Pocket!

Jaggers There's no "of course" about it: he is, or he is not. Now attend to me, if you please. Your name occurs pretty often in Wemmick's cash book. You have been drawing freely and you are in debt, are you no?

Pip I'm afraid I must say yes, sir.

Jaggers You know you must say yes, don't you?

Pip Yes, sir.

Jaggers Very well. (*Drily*) Debt is the mark of a gentleman. (*He produces a banknote*) Now take this piece of paper in your hand.

Pip takes the note

You have it? Unfold it and tell me what it is.

Pip (*obeying*) This is a banknote for five hundred pounds.

Jaggers That is a banknote for five hundred pounds. And a very handsome sum of money too, I think. You consider it so?

Pip How could I do otherwise?

Jaggers Ah! But answer the question.

Pip Undoubtedly.

Jaggers You consider it, undoubtedly, a handsome sum of money. And at the rate of that handsome sum of money per annum, and at no higher sum, you are to live until your benefactor appears. (*Before Pip can answer, he repeats his earlier caveat*) Which may be years hence.

Herbert looks doleful

(*Looking at Herbert*) Mr Pocket, you do not rejoice on your friend's behalf?

Herbert Oh, I do, most assuredly, Handel. If I seem glum, it is because every day I go into the city and look about me, and as long as I look and as hard as I look, I don't think I shall ever look upon five hundred pounds.

Pip Your luck will change, Herbert. I'm sure of it.

Herbert That's what Clara, brave girl, keeps telling me. Do you know, I have seven siblings, and I am the only one of them who is engaged.

Pip Really? But bravo, then! Well done.

Herbert Not really. All the others — excepting the baby — are married. I begin to despair — I truly do ...

A carriage clock is heard striking the half hour

Jaggers Gentlemen, I am sorry to announce it is half-past nine, and we must break up. Go to see Wemmick tomorrow, Pip. That — handsome sum of yours is to be signed for.

SCENE 2

The Lights fade on Jaggers' house, leaving the DS area lit

Pip moves DS. Young Pip stands close by

This scene is played entirely to the audience

Pip The generosity of my unnamed benefactor implanted a seed in my mind. I had for some time wished to be of assistance to Herbert. Those on whom fortune has smiled should think of others..
Young Pip That is the nature of a gentleman.
Pip (*ignoring this*) Herbert was after all my first and best and truest London friend. He had taught me all that was important.
Young Pip Table manners.
Pip To raise my hat on meeting a lady.
Young Pip Not to drop an aitch at one end of a word and not to drop a "g" at the other.
Pip He taught me about art.
Young Pip And the playhouse.
Pip How to converse gracefully.
Young Pip How to order a dinner.
Pip Where to be seen and where not to be seen.
Young Pip How to be in the fashion.
Pip And yet Herbert was never a snob. Never did he seek to inculcate that quality in me.
Young Pip I learned that all by myself.

Pip stiffens, offended

SCENE 3

The Lights cross-fade to Wemmick's office. Wemmick is on his high stool

Pip moves to Wemmick

Pip Mr Wemmick ...
Wemmick Mr Pip, hallo.
Pip I want to ask your opinion. I am very desirous to serve a friend.

Wemmick shakes his head

This friend is trying to get on in commercial life, but has no money. I want somehow to help him to a beginning.
Wemmick With money down?
Pip With *some* money down, and perhaps some drawing upon my expectations ...
Wemmick Mr Pip, I should just like to run over with you the names of the various bridges up as high as Chelsea Reach.

Pip The bridges?

Wemmick If you please. Let's see; there's London, one; Southwark, two;
  Blackfriars, three; Waterloo, four; Westminster, five; Vauxhall, six. Six to
  choose from.

Pip I don't understand you.

Wemmick Choose your bridge, Mr Pip, and take a walk upon your bridge,
  and pitch your money into the Thames over the centre arch of your bridge
  and you know the end of it. Serve a friend, and you may know the end of
  it, too, but it's a less present and profitable end.

Pip This is very discouraging.

Wemmick Meant to be so.

Pip Then you say that a man should never ——

Wemmick — invest portable property in a friend? Never, unless he wishes
  to get rid of the friend.

Pip And that is your deliberate opinion.

Wemmick That is my deliberate opinion in this office.

Pip Ah! In this ...?

Wemmick My home in Walworth is one place, and this office is another,
  much as the Aged is one person and Mr Jaggers is another. My Walworth
  sentiments must be taken at Walworth.

Pip Then may we converse at Walworth?

Wemmick (*climbing down from his stool*) With the greatest pleasure, Mr
  Pip. As you have found out, Mr Jaggers gives you wine and good wine. I'll
  give you punch, and not bad punch. Will it please you to walk with me to
  Walworth?

SCENE 4

*Pip and Wemmick walk towards Wemmick's home, the Lights cross-fading
to follow them*

*A Light comes up on the Aged Parent in his chair and making toast with the
aid of a toasting-fork. He wears a flannel coat and is very old and "clean,
cheerful, comfortable." A Union Jack flies over his head and perhaps there
is a cut-out plywood battlement. Under the flag and by the Aged P.'s ear there
is a small cannon*

Pip and Wemmick arrive at Wemmick's home

Wemmick Here we are, Mr Pip. Take care, mind how you cross the moat.
  I like to think that if an Englishman's home is his castle, it should have the
  civility to *look* like a castle. Every evening at sunset, I take down the flag
  and fire the gun. Being deaf, the Aged likes that.

Pip, followed by Wemmick, picks his steps carefully as if crossing a rickety plank

Well done, Mr Pip. One day, see if I don't, I'll put water in that moat. Well, Aged Parent, how are you?

Aged P.   All right, John. All right.

Wemmick Here's Mr Pip, Aged Parent, and I wish you could hear his name. Nod away at him, Mr Pip. That's what he likes. Nod away, like winking!

Pip and the Aged P. launch into an exchange of massive nods

Aged P.   This is a fine place of my son's, sir. This spot ought to be kept by the nation, after my son's time, for the people's enjoyment.

Wemmick You're as proud of it as Punch, ain't you, Aged? *There's* a nod for you. *There's* another for you! If you're not tired, Mr Pip, will you tip him one more? You can't think how it pleases him.

Pip nods to the Aged P., then turns to the audience

Pip   (*to the audience*) Walking from Mr Jaggers' office, Wemmick's habitual dryness and hardness had fallen away. By the time we had crossed the Thames it was quite gone, and he had devised a plan to assist Herbert to a small income by stealth.

Wemmick Leave it to me. I'll put on my considering-cap, and Miss Skiffins' brother is an accountant. He'll help us.

Pip   Miss Skiffins?

Wemmick She comes of an evening. I place my arm around her waist, you know.

Pip   Do you?

Wemmick Oh, yes. At first, Miss Skiffins affects not to notice. Then, bless her, she looks down, sees what I'm about, unwinds my arm as if it were a girdle and puts my hand on the table.

Pip   And — may I ask — what then?

Wemmick Then? Why then it begins all over again. What evenings we have, eh, Aged Parent?

There is more nodding. During the following, the Aged P. dozes off

Now! (*He puts a finger to his lips, then goes to the little flagstaff and lowers the Union Jack*) Yes, give me a week or so, and I wouldn't be at all surprised if your friend, Mr Pocket, should hear from a young merchant or shipping broker who's in need of a partner.

Pip I thank you ten thousand times.

Wemmick No, I thank *you*. I deal over-much in criminality, and this will blow the Newgate cobwebs away. (*He takes the hot toasting fork from the nodding Aged P.*) Begging your pardon, Aged Parent. (*He touches the tip of the fork to the powder in the cannon*)

The cannon goes off with a great explosion and a vast cloud of smoke. Pip, caught unawares, claps his hands to his ears and goes reeling

Aged P. (*waking*) Was that it, John? Did it go off?

The Lights go down

ACT VI
Magwitch Returns

Scene 1

Sounds of wind and storm

A Light comes up on Young Pip

Young Pip A year passed, and another, and I was — *he* was — was twenty-three years of age. Not one word had he heard on the subject of his expectations. Him and me, him the gentleman and me that worked for Joe Gargery the blacksmith — me and him, we no longer kept close company.

The Lights come up on Pip in his rooms reading a book at a table, lit by a lamp

There was a night of storm, with mud, mud, mud, deep in all the streets. The lamps on the bridges were shivering, and the coal fires in the barges on the river were being carried away before the wind like red-hot splashes in the rain.

Pip Who is there? (*He rises with the lamp.*) There is someone there, is there not?

Magwitch (*off*) Someone is here.

Pip What floor do you want?

Magwitch (*off*) The top. Mr Pip.

Pip That is my name. There is nothing the matter?

Magwitch (*off*) Nothing the matter.

Magwitch appears, a man of sixty, dressed like a seafarer. He sees Pip and extends both hands towards him, giving a great sigh of contentment

Magwitch It's you, then!

Pip Pray, what is your business?

Magwitch My business? I'll speak in half a minute. Give me half a minute.

Pip No. Say it now. Why do you, a stranger, come into my rooms at this time of night?

Magwitch (*chuckling*) You're a game 'un. I'm glad you've growed up a game 'un. And you was a game 'un then them years ago on the meshes.

Pip (*knowing*) Who are you?

Magwitch You acted noble, my boy. Noble Pip! And I have never forgot it!

Pip You! My — my convict.

Magwitch (*attempting to embrace him*) Yes! And you are my own dear noble boy.

Pip Oh, my God. No — stay. Keep off. My poor man, if you are grateful for what I once did, if you have come here to thank me, it is not necessary. I do not repulse you, never that, but you must — must understand — I —— (*He breaks off, quailing under Magwitch's look*)

Magwitch Say on, Master. What is it that this warmint must understand?

Pip Why, that I cannot wish to renew my acquaintance with you of long ago. If I deserve to be thanked, I am glad. But let us bear in mind that our ways, yours and mine, are different ways.

Magwitch Different ways.

Pip Yes. But you are wet, and you look weary. Will you drink something before you go?

Magwitch I think that I *will* drink — I thank you — before I go.

Magwitch sits. Pip finds two glasses and a bottle of brandy. He pours a glass for Magwitch and the latter downs it in a single swallow. Pip refills the glass

Pip I hope you will not think I spoke harshly to you just now. I am sorry if I did. I wish you well, and happy. (*Pause*) Might I ask how you are living?

Magwitch Why, I've been a sheep farmer, stock-breeder, other trades besides, away in the New World.

Pip Indeed. I hope you have done well.

Magwitch I've done wonderfully well. I'm famous for it.

Pip I am glad to hear it. Nonetheless, I hope you will not be offended. (*He produces his purse and takes from it two one-pound notes*)

Magwitch Two pounds! No offence in the wide world, dear boy. (*He folds the banknotes lengthwise and casually burns them in the flame of the lamp during the following*) And may a warmint make so bold as to ask if you have prospered since you and me was out on them lone shivering meshes?

Pip Prospered?

Magwitch Done well.

Pip I have been chosen to succeed to some property.

Magwitch Might a mere warmint ask what property?
Pip I don't know.
Magwitch Might a mere warmint ask whose property?
Pip (*faltering*) I don't know.
Magwitch Might a mere warmint make a guess as to your income since you
   come of age? As to the first figure now. Five?

Pip stares at Magwitch with increasing horror

   Concerning a guardian — a lawyer, maybe. As to the first letter of that
   lawyer's name now. Would it be J?

Pip starts up, overturning his chair

   (*Rising*) Yes, Pip, dear boy, I've made a gentleman on you! It's me what
   has done it. I swore that time, sure as ever I earned a guinea, that guinea
   should go to you. I lived rough, that you should live smooth. I worked hard,
   that you should be above work. This here hunted dunghill dog what you
   kep' life in, got his head so high that he could make a gentleman. And, Pip,
   you're him!

Magwitch seizes Pip's hand and holds it up so that a finger-ring is visible

   Look 'ee here! A diamond all set round with rubies; that's a gentleman's,
   I hope! Look at your linen, fine and beautiful! Look at your clothes, better
   ain't to be got! You been reading a book; you shall read to me, dear boy.

Pip is silent

   (*Laughing*) Don't you pay heed to a warmint's foolish words. You ain't
   looked forward to this as I have. But didn't you never think it might be me?
Pip No. Never — never.
Magwitch Well, you see it was me, and single-handed.
Pip Was there no-one else?
Magwitch Who else should there be? And, dear boy, how handsome you
   have growed. There's bright eyes somewheres, eh? Isn't there bright eyes
   somewheres wot you love the thoughts on? Speak out. Them eyes shall be
   yourn, dear boy, if money can buy 'em. Not that a gentleman like you can't
   win 'em at his own game. And now — where will you put me?
Pip Put you?
Magwitch Ay. I been sea-tossed and sea-washed months and months. And
   look 'ee here. Not a word outside these walls. For by God, it's death.
Pip What do you mean?

Magwitch I was sent for life. It's death to come back, and if took, I should of a certainty be 'anged.

Pip Then this is madness. You cannot stay.

Magwitch Dear boy, I'm an old bird, as 'as dared all manner of traps, and I ain't afeerd to perch on a scarecrow. If there's death inside, then let him come out and I'll face him. I'm with my boy now, and I've come for good.

Pip For good?

Herbert enters

Herbert Handel, there never has been such a night. They say there's not a chimney-pot in London that isn't——(*He breaks off on seeing Magwitch*)

Magwitch at once becomes menacing and produces an open jack-knife

Pip This is Mr Pocket, my dear friend. Herbert, this is an unexpected visitor.

Herbert (*staring at the knife and the visitor*) How do you do?

Magwitch (*producing a prayer book from his pocket*) Take this in your right hand. Take it, I say. Lord strike you dead on the spot if you split in any way some-ever. Kiss it! Lord ——

Herbert (*terrified*) — strike me dead on the spot.

Magwitch And now you're on your oath, boy. And never believe me on mine if one of these days Pip shan't make a gentleman of you!

Pip Herbert, I must go and talk with Mr Jaggers.

Herbert Now? Do you mean I am to be left with ...?

Pip (*to Magwitch*) What do you call yourself? You assumed some name, I suppose, on board ship.

Magwitch Yes, dear boy. I took the name of Provis.

Pip What is your real name?

Magwitch Magwitch. Christened Abel.

Pip Abel Magwitch. I have business in Gerrard Street. You may have trust in my friend, as you have trust in me. If you have trust in me.

Magwitch If I have trust in you ... !

Magwitch makes as if to embrace Pip, who holds him off, backing away

Herbert Handel, for pity's sake ...

Pip Forgive me. I have a question that Mr Jaggers and no-one else can answer.

Pip moves to Jaggers'

Herbert (*alone with Magwitch*) I too have a question. Am I destined to see the light of dawn?

Magwitch sits at the table across from Herbert. He pours a glass of brandy and with deliberation places his jack-knife on the table. Herbert is very frightened

SCENE 2

The Lights cross-fade to Jaggers' room. Jaggers and Pip are there

Jaggers Now, Pip, be careful.

Pip I will, sir. I merely want, Mr Jaggers, to assure myself that what I have been told is true.

Jaggers Did you say "told" or "informed"? Told would seem to imply verbal communication. You cannot have verbal communication with a man in New South Wales, you know.

Pip I will say informed, Mr Jaggers.

Jaggers Good.

Pip I have been informed by a man named Abel Magwitch that he is the benefactor so long unknown to me.

Jaggers That is the man in New South Wales.

Pip And only he?

Jaggers And only he.

Pip I am not so unreasonable, sir, as to think you responsible for my mistakes and wrong conclusions, but I always supposed it to be Miss Havisham.

Jaggers As you say, Pip, I am not responsible for that.

Pip And yet it looked so like it, sir.

Jaggers Not a particle of evidence, Pip. Take nothing on its looks; take everything on evidence. There is no better rule.

Molly (*off*) Master? Have you need of me?

Jaggers (*calling*) No, Molly. I have had a late caller. You may go to bed. Good-night, Pip.

SCENE 3

The Lights cross-fade to Pip's rooms

Jaggers exits

Magwitch Have I had an interestin life, young sir? I been in jail and out of jail since I was a little'un. Yes, I think a Gentleman might call that of passing interest.

Herbert Most inconvenient for you, I'm sure.

Magwitch I'm obliged to hear you say so, sir. Not that I'm a varmant who's ever been given to complaint. I been beaten for doing what was wrong and I been kicked for doing what was right, so I ought to be grateful to the world for according me the honour of being impartial. And I've had vittles, and I've gone without vittles. You harken to me, young gentlemen; never, if you can help it, go short of vittles, for out of a disinclination to starve, you might, as I did, fall in with a bad 'un. Worse than bad, damn his eyes, and worse than worse! Oh, that name, that name, may it echo in hell. Com-pey-son!

Herbert Compeyson?

Magwitch You know him? You've heard of him?

Herbert (*frightened*) No ... never.

Magwitch His business was swindling and forgery, and he made his business mine. When he was caught and put on trial, he betrayed me to save his own skin. Compeyson!

Pip appears, listening in silence

My boy, you've come back.

Pip Yes, and we must find you a place to sleep.

Herbert Let him have my bed, for I shall not sleep tonight.

Pip Come then.

Herbert Handel, did you hear what he said? The man Compeyson, his accomplice, his enemy — don't you remember? Compeyson is the man who five-and-twenty years ago was Miss Havisham's lover ——

The Lights cross-fade to the Satis House area. During the following, Magwitch and Herbert exit

ACT VII
Departure

SCENE 1

Miss Havisham and Estella are visible in the Satis House area. There are lighted candles around them

Miss Havisham Speak the truth, you ingrate. This man. This villain. You'll marry him to spite me. Confess it!

Estella Will you deny me that small pleasure?

Miss Havisham Oh, you stick and stone. You cold, cold heart.

Estella What? Do you reproach me for being cold? You?

Miss Havisham Are you not?

Estella I am what you have made me. Say, then: what you want from me?

Miss Havisham Love.

Estella You have it.

Miss Havisham I have not. So hard, so hard.

Estella Who taught me to be hard?

Miss Havisham Hard, and proud as well. And thankless. She to whom I gave
my name. She whom I took into this wretched breast when it was still
bleeding from its stabs. I gave her a name when she had none, I gave her
a life when she had none. I gave her expectations.
Estella Expectations ...
Miss Havisham Yes!
Estella Yes. And now they are fulfilled. Be happy, then. The fruit of your
scheming is about to be ——
Miss Havisham You devil ... Viper ...

Pip comes into the room. Both women fall silent

Pip Estella?
Estella Pip!
Miss Havisham (*with a disdainful look at Estella*) Well, Pip, what wind
blows you here?
Pip A bitter wind, Miss Havisham. I have found out who my patron is.
Miss Havisham So?
Pip It is not a fortunate discovery, nor is it likely ever to enrich me in
reputation or in fortune.
Miss Havisham These are sad tidings, Pip.
Pip I know now that when first I came here, it was as any other poor boy might
have come, as a kind of servant, to gratify a want or a whim, and be paid
at the end of it.
Miss Havisham Ay, Pip, so you did.
Pip Then, when Mr Jaggers ——
Miss Havisham Pray leave Mr Jaggers out of it. His being my lawyer and
the lawyer of your patron is a coincidence. The mistake was not of his
doing.
Pip No, it was mine. All the same, you led me on.
Miss Havisham Yes! I let you go on.
Pip Why? Was that kind?
Miss Havisham Kind? (*Passionately*) Who am I, for God's sake, that I
should be kind? Answer me!
Pip Forgive me. I am presumptuous. I have no right to ask of you what was
never in you to give.
Miss Havisham Now he is impudent. Estella, do you hear? The blacksmith's
boy upbraids me.
Estella Pip, I am sorry to see you unhappy. And I wish you had not come here
today. You give me no choice but to say what you would not hear. I am to
be married within the week.
Pip (*after a pause*) Is it to Bentley Drummle?
Estella Yes.

Pip Then it is what I feared most of all. That you would fling yourself away on a brute.

Estella At least don't be afraid of my being a blessing to him. Miss Havisham would have me wait, and not marry yet. Besides, Mr Drummle is too coarse for her liking. She would have me choose a kindlier, gentler husband. Then his pain would give her a more satisfying revenge upon all men. (*To Miss Havisham*) Is that not so?

Miss Havisham Base ingratitude! I'll not suffer it. Marry him, then. Marry whoever you please. Betray me. (*She seizes up a lighted candle from the dressing table*)

Estella Pip, you will be none the worse for this. It will pass.

Pip Never.

Estella You will get me out of your thoughts in a week. (*She offers Pip her hand*) Here now, let us part friends.

Miss Havisham faces US *and unmasks a powerful amber light which shines through her dress and hair; this produces the effect of the candles igniting Miss Havisham's dress. There is a series of screams, each one more piercing, more terror-filled than the one before*

Estella *Moth-er!*

Black-out

Estella, Miss Havisham and Pip exit

SCENE 2

The Lights come up on Wemmick's home

The Aged Parent is in his chair, dozing and holding his toasting fork

Wemmick comes in, home from work. He carries a small package containing sausages

Wemmick There you are, Aged Parent. How are you? Are you as right as rain, then?

Aged P. No, no, I'm all right, my boy.

Wemmick Here's a handshake for you. And a nod. And another nod. And a sausage for you to toast. The world would turn the other way if you didn't have your sausage! (*He takes a sausage from his package and impales it on the end of the toasting fork*) Have at that, then. So what news, Aged P.? Has Mr Pip come? (*Loudly*) I say, is Mr Pip here?

Aged P. No, never that. It's your Mr Pip come a-visiting.

Pip (*off*) Mr Wemmick.

Pip enters. One of his hands is roughly bandaged

I was enjoying your garden and thought I heard your voice.

Wemmick I imagine all of Walworth heard my voice. Then you received my
note.

Pip "Don't come home." Most alarming.

Wemmick Meant to be alarming. Home ... is that where our friend is?

Pip Do you mean Mag ——

Wemmick No names Mr Pip. Walls have ears, even if the Aged P. does not.

Pip (*affirming*) Our friend shares with me. Herbert has taken lodgings
nearby.

Wemmick Not good. Dangerous. Our friend must be moved. Tonight, in
darkness.

Pip Do you mean he is being watched?

Wemmick Let us say sought after.

Pip So soon? Mr Wemmick, do you know of a man of bad character, name
of Compeyson?

Wemmick The police spy? The informer? I do.

Pip Is he in London?

Wemmick He's the one. Now go warily, Mr Pip. Don't break cover too soon.
Wait before you try for foreign parts.

Pip Foreign parts?

Wemmick He can't stay in England, Mr Pip. That bandage has come loose.
Let me attend to it. And could you spare a nod to the Aged?

Pip By all means.

*An exchange of nods. Pip sits and Wemmick reties the bandage during the
following*

Aged P. Come and warm your hands by the fire, Mr Pip.

Wemmick You don't look well, Mr Pip. Your attempt — valiant as it was,
in vain as it was, to save the poor lady was not without cost.

Pip Mr Wemmick, about our man...

Wemmick Shh! Shh!

Pip Our friend. *Was* it a coincidence? I mean, that Mr Jaggers should have
been his lawyer and Miss Havisham's as well?

Wemmick Well, is it a coincidence, Mr Pip, if two gentlemen of fashion go
to the same tailor? It was at a time when Mr Jaggers had come into his own.
He had defended a gypsy woman on a charge of murder. All of London
begged to be his client.

Pip She was acquitted?

Wemmick It was alleged that she had killed another woman of her sort, that jealousy was at the back of it. There were deep scars on her hands.

Pip starts

Did I hurt you?

Pip Scars on her hands, you say?

Wemmick Mr Jaggers argued as how they were not caused by fingernails but by brambles. It was also alleged that in madness she had destroyed her own child by the man in the case, to be revenged on him. "Prove it," Mr Jaggers said. "Prove that such a child exists." Well, the jury gave in. He was too many for them.

Pip "A wild beast tamed."

Wemmick Beg pardon?

Pip Mr Jaggers' housekeeper. She is the woman.

Wemmick Well done, that's her. He said he took her in as what you might call a trophy. I think myself it was goodness of heart, but being charitable, I wouldn't accuse him of something so unnatural.

Pip Mr Wemmick ...

Wemmick (*finished with the bandage*) There. That'll do, I think.

Pip About the child.

Wemmick Child? What child would that be? She never existed.

Pip *She*, Mr Wemmick?

Wemmick She, Mr Pip.

SCENE 3

Jaggers enters, facing front. During the following, Pip and Wemmick will come forward, facing front

Jaggers Put this case, Pip. That a lawyer held a trust to find a child for an eccentric rich lady to adopt and bring up. Put the cases Pip, that the lawyer habitually saw children tried at a criminal bar. That he knew of their being imprisoned, whipped, cast out, qualified in all ways for the hangman and growing up to be hanged. Put the case that there was one pretty little child out of the heap that could be saved. Put the case that the lawyer said to the child's mother: "I know what you did and how you did it. Give the child into my hands and I'll do my best to get you off. If I save you, your child is saved. If you are lost, the child is still saved." Put that case to yourself, and mind that the lawyer makes no admissions. Well, Mr Pip?

Pip The lawyer did right.

Jaggers Never mind what is right, sir. Stick to the law. Wemmick?

Wemmick No admissions, no case to answer.

Jaggers Just so. *Nolle prosequi*, I think? (*i.e. the matter has been argued and disposed of*) Wemmick, I was not aware until I spoke today with Mr Pip that all these years you have an old father and a most pleasant home.

Wemmick Well?

Jaggers *You* with a pleasant home? You must be the most cunning impostor in all London.

Wemmick The *second* most cunning impostor.

Jaggers, bested, goes off on his dignity

Scene 4

The Lights cross-fade to Pip's lodgings. Herbert enters and waits for Pip

Wemmick and Pip shake hands and go in separate directions

Wemmick exits

Pip goes into his lodgings

Pip Where is he?

Herbert Getting ready. Another minute and we shall be on our way. But my dear Handel, you seem ill.

Pip I think I was followed.

Herbert What? (*He comes* DS *and looks out*)

Pip Perhaps I take fright at shadows. At any rate, we must make a run for it. Our best course is to take him downriver to Gravesend. Tomorrow we can row out to midstream and hail the packet for Rotterdam.

Herbert Handel, I think I know Magwitch by now. He has come a long way, and he will not go back.

Pip He will if I go with him.

Herbert Go with him? On your life you must not.

Pip He risked his life to come here and find me. All of his fortune was for me, and much good did I make of it. Joe Gargery in his forge is more a gentleman than I shall ever be.

Herbert is about to protest

I have manners and I have affectations, and until Magwitch revealed himself I had five hundred pounds a year. No, Herbert, being an upstart and being a gentleman are not quite the same thing.

Herbert You know that if he is taken, all that he has will be forfeit to the Crown.

Pip Do you think I can ever again touch a penny of it? His money has brought me nothing but unhappiness, and has cost me the only family I ever knew.

Herbert Then how will you live? Now pray, don't be offended, but my partner and I manage to rub along in a modest way, and — dare I say it? —we have room for a clerk. You would be poorly paid at first, but if we prosper ——

Pip laughs

Is it so laughable?

Pip Not at all ...

Herbert Say yes, then ...

During the following, Young Pip appears outside

Pip All I have ever attempted to keep hold of, I have lost. I smile now because whatever few coins I have given away, they are still mine! Thank you, dear friend, but I must go with Magwitch. Perhaps he and I will —— (*His attention is caught by Young Pip*)

Herbert What is it?

Pip That boy again.

Herbert The scowling youth who follows you about? Is he watching us?

Pip Yes. But no longer scowling.

The Lights cross-fade to a small wharf on the river. A boat is tied to the wharf; this is represented by no more than a bowpiece. Fog swirls about

Magwitch is waiting; he raises a mast as the Lights change

Young Pip exits

Magwitch I'm ready, dear boy. You may do with me what you will.

Pip Magwitch before we leave here, I must warn you. We are in grave danger. There is a man whose name is Compeyson ——

Magwitch (*in sullen rage*) Him? Him, do you say?

Pip He is leading the police to you. Even now escape may be too late.

Magwitch To the devil with escape. Let me get these hands on him, and I'll kiss whatever gibbet I swing from.

Pip Magwitch, listen to me. You must choose now either to die or to live. Tomorrow, if our luck holds, you can be out of England, and I shall be with you.

Magwitch (*overjoyed*) You? You would go with me?

Pip I, to seek my fortune; you, to enjoy yours. There's my hand on it. (*He offers his hand to Magwitch*)

Magwitch (*shaking Pip's hand*) Oh, he's a rare 'un! I allus knowed. From that day on the marshes I knowed there warn't his equal.

Pip Now we must go. (*He gets into the boat, swaying*)

Magwitch Dear boy, thankee. I declare there's justice after all, this side o' heaven. I never thought a round score o' year ago, that when I seen the last o' one dear child I'd mebbe some day find 'er equal ...

Pip (*to Magwitch*) *You* lost a child, you say?

Magwitch Not lost, was robbed. A little girl. That were how I knew to take up wi' Mr Jaggers. Because it were him that got her off, you see — her, my woman, he saved her. And arterwards, for me there were no more of her or of the little 'un. Swallyed up, gone, the both of 'em, dear boy.

Pip Swallowed up, yes. And so now at last we have the truth of it. Magwitch, hear me. Whatever befalls us, know this.

Magwitch Dear boy ...

Pip The child that was lost — your daughter — lived. She is living now. She is a lady and very beautiful. And the least and most of it is, I love her.

Magwitch Living, you say? My child, my girl. Alive, you say? For that I'd give my life and smile doing it. Let the river take me. Now I'm the world's master.

A flash of lightning. A roll of thunder

Herbert Now, go — for pity's sake, go.

Magwitch and Herbert get into the boat; Pip rows

A ship's siren sounds, deep and urgent

SCENE 5

The Lights go out on the wharf; the boat is now on the open water

A Voice Ahoy, there! Avast! You have a returned transport there. Abel Magwitch, otherwise Provis, I call on you to surrender!

Magwitch Compeyson!

Again the siren is heard. There is discord, lightning and thunder as the small boat and its occupants are lost in the river. This is not an attempt to create real action, but rather to reflect the disorder of Pip's mind

Black-out; silence

SCENE 6

The Lights come up slowly

Pip is in an invalid chair. He seems to be asleep. Joe is with him

Pip's head moves

Pip Herbert? Herbert, where are you? Are you there? Herbert? Is there no-one to hear me?

Joe Hallo, are you awake then, Pip?

Pip Joe? Is it you?

Joe Which it air, old chap.

Pip Or is it another dream? I've had so many dreams, some of them of you, Joe. If it really *is* you, look angry at me. Please...no kindness.

Joe Which dear old Pip, you and me was ever friends. And when you're well enough to come to Biddy and me — oh then, what larks!

Pip Where is Herbert, Joe? Is he here?

Joe Him? Which he's been took foreign, Pip, on business.

Pip And so you are here, tending to me in his place.

Joe "Go to him," Biddy says, when the news came of your being took so ill, "go to him without a minute's loss of time." Such were the word of Biddy.

Pip So many dreams, Joe. Of Miss Havisham. Of Estella. Of you. And of the river.

Joe That were real, Pip. The river were real. And me. I make bold to say that I were real.

Pip And Magwitch. What of Magwitch? Joe, be truthful. He is dead, isn't he?

Joe Why, you see, old chap, I wouldn't go so far as to say that, for that's a deal to say; but he ain't ——

Pip Living, Joe?

Joe That's nearer to where he is. He ain't living, Pip.

Pip No dream this time, Joe?

Joe Wide awake, old chap.

Pip I see us, as clear as clear: Magwitch, Herbert and I, rowing out to the deep channel to hail the packet. No sooner did we have sight of her than there came another boat, bearing down on us.

Joe No dream neither, Pip.

Pip Calling out for Magwitch to surrender. And he looked, and in that other boat he saw his mortal enemy. Compeyson!

Joe Still no dream, Pip.

Pip Then the other boat came upon us. And there were two men in the water. Struggling and swept beneath the great wheel of the packet. Joe, did they both perish?

Joe Drownded, both, Pip. Long gone past dreaming.

Pip Magwitch dead. And all because of me. All because one day a boy stole
food to help a starving man. And Joe, I thought, too, as clear as life itself,
I thought that Estella came here to visit me, and spoke kind and tender
words and stroked my forehead. Was that so?

Joe Which that *were* a dream, Pip.

Pip Well, you at least are real, Joe. And I am undeserving.

Joe Pip, there has been larks. And, dear sir, what have been betwixt us, have
been.

Wemmick appears

Wemmick Well, bravo, Mr Pip. I see you are much improved.

Pip Mr Wemmick, how good of you ...

Wemmick Today I have a mind to take a holiday. Is Mr Pip well enough,
do you think, Mr Gargery, to be taken out of doors?

Joe Which, sir, I meantersay that Pip might as well smell the fresh air as be
sittin' here having dreams of it, which makes no differ in any case such as
it being only London fresh air and not much better than none.

Wemmick Good. Let us walk to Camberwell, then.

Pip Camberwell? Why, what is in Camberwell?

Wemmick We soon shall be.

SCENE 7

*Wemmick and Joe have a small battle to take charge of the invalid chair,
which Joe, being the stronger, wins. They walk*

Wemmick And indeed here we are. Well, Mr Pip, how do you feel?

Pip Why, I confess I'm glad to be alive.

Wemmick I'm not surprised. It is a common sensation in Camberwell. (*He
stops*) Hallo! Here's a church.

Pip (*bemused*) Well, so I see.

Wemmick And hallo! Here's gloves. (*He takes two pairs of white kid gloves
from his pocket*) Let's put them on.

Pip Mr Wemmick, what on earth ——

Wemmick And hallo once more! There's the Aged P.!

*The Aged Parent appears, beaming, a flower in his buttonhole. A veiled
female figure moves into sight wearing a wedding dress*

And hallo! There's Miss ——

Pip (*starting in terror*) No. No, it cannot be!

Joe What is it, Pip old chap?

Pip Is it Miss Havisham?

Wemmick Bless your heart, no, Mr Pip. It's Miss Skiffins. (*He affects surprise*) Miss Skiffins? And hallo again! (*He produces a ring from his pocket*) Here's a ring! Let's have a wedding.

Miss Skiffins takes Wemmick's arm and they all head for the exit in procession, followed by the Aged Parent

EPILOGUE

Scene 1

Wemmick (*addressing the audience*) Weddings do happen, you know, and except in tragedies a wedding is a story's end.

Wemmick, Miss Skiffins, Joe and the Aged P. exit

Pip gets out of his chair and walks forward

Pip What is to become of me?

Young Pip Well? What is to become of you?

Young Pip enters and gives Pip a book. Pip opens it

Pip (*opening the book*) What's this then?

Young Pip grins at Pip

Eh? (*He reads, intrigued*) Chapter the Last! Saucy young devil. Why, I am to be a clerk in Herbert's company. Well done! I shall ... But surely not. I must quit England and for nine years make my home abroad, live frugally and pay my debts.

Young Pip Your debts? You have none. While you were ill, did Joe not pay all you owe?

Pip So I at last discovered. And dear Joe, who has ever and always returned good for evil, is he not himself to be repaid? (*He reads*) I shall work hard — (*He skims through the pages, mumbling*) — mmm ... mmm ... and be put in sole charge of the Eastern Branch and one day hope to become a partner. A third in the house. (*He discovers good tidings*) In time I shall return to England and live contentedly — more or less — with Herbert and his wife Clara.

Young Pip Until one day ——

Pip — there will come word from dear Joe. I shall be sent for.

Pip closes the book and gives it to Young Pip

Young Pip (*to the audience*) Weddings do happen, you know, and except
    in tragedies a wedding is a story's end. I was to be ... (*he corrects himself*)
    Mr Pip was to be ——
Pip We were to be ——
Young Pip — the best man.

SCENE 2

*Biddy, wearing a white wedding dress, enters with Joe. Pip and she regard
each other, smiling*

Pumblechook enters showering Biddy, Joe and Pip with rice

Pumblechook May I ? May I? May I?
Pip No, sir. You may not!
Pumblechook (*sternly*) This is him as I have rode in my shay! This is him
    as I have seen brought up by hand. This is him as has showed his benefactor
    the basest ingratititood. (*sic*)
Pip I swear, look as I may, I see no benefactor before me, sir.
Pumblechook And *I* swear you will see him behind you, sir!

   Pumblechook strides off, mortally offended

Pip goes to Biddy. They embrace

Biddy Pip ... Dear Pip ... I'm so happy.
Pip And you will make Joe as happy as he deserves to be.
Joe Oh, Pip. Don't say that, for since I have never been of much consequence,
    then I should, I'm sure, be miserable.
Biddy Joe! I have the best husband in the world.
Pip And he has the best wife. And who knows? One day some little fellow
    will come to sit in the chimney corner of a winter night.
Biddy Pip!
Joe What little fellow?
Biddy Joe!
Pip And he may remind you, Joe, of another little fellow gone out of it
    forever. And if so, be kind. Don't tell him I was thankless.
Joe Pip. Old chap!
Biddy And what of you, Pip? Are you happy?
Pip Yes. And to forestall your other question, I am quite the old bachelor.
Biddy For shame, then!

Pip Mind, I have dreams.

Biddy (*smiling*) Not surely of again becoming a gentleman?

Pip Which, you know, I never did. No, I mean that I still dream as I did long ago when I was ill. There are times when the past and the present and what is to come seem all one to me.

Biddy Well, perhaps they *are* all one.

Pip Do you think so? Yesternight, I dreamt that I met Estella on a street in London. That she was older and much changed, as perhaps I am. And we shook hands and wished each other well and parted.

Biddy Do you know of Estella?

Pip Nothing.

Biddy And was she married in your dream, Pip?

Pip looks at Biddy

Because, you know, she is not married out of it.

Pip (*in surprise*) Biddy!

Joe A village has few secrets, Pip. Not at all like London.

Biddy Estella swore that she would have none of Miss Havisham's estate. Perhaps she wished at last to be free of her. At any rate Satis House is to be pulled down. They say ——

Joe You know how they gossip ...

Biddy Joe! They say that your Estella lives there, the better to take leave of it.

Pip She lives there. And not married, you say? But why?

Biddy I'm sure I don't know. But I'm sure she does.

Pip kisses Biddy's cheek and goes towards Satis House

Joe enters and takes his place beside Biddy. They stand with Young Pip as a threesome

Scene 3

A Light comes on in the Satis House area and Estella is there, older now. She sees Pip

Biddy Do you think it is true, Joe, that what is past and present and yet still to come are all one?

Young Pip Do you, Joe?

Joe signs for them to be quiet

Pip Estella!

Estella You here? Pip? I wonder that you know me. You stare. Am I so different?

Pip Forgive me. I cannot believe it. They say you are not married after all.

Estella They say true then. I renounced Miss Havisham's estate, you know.

Pip Yes, I ——

Estella And the man I was to marry ——

Pip Bentley Drummle ...

Estella Was that his name? Then for his part, he could do no less than pay me the compliment of renouncing me. And you, Pip. Do you come so that we may say goodbye yet again? For if so, then let us continue friends apart. (*She offers her hand*)

Pip (*taking Estella's hand*) I see no shadow of another parting.

Estella (*smiling*) Dear Pip, I do despair of you. Will you never take heed?

Young Pip Answer Biddy, Joe. What has been, and what is still to be. Are they all one?

Joe (*putting an arm around Biddy, his other arm around the shoulder of the young Pip*) Biddy ... Pip, old chap, which in answer I meantersay that what have been betwixt us, have been.

THE END

FURNITURE AND PROPERTY LIST

PART I

Mrs Joe: Thin cane
Table. *On it*: loaf of bread, pat of butter, knife
Benches
Large bottle
In "pantry" : bread, cheese, pork pie, bottle of brandy
Pumblechook: bottle of sherry, bottle of port
Glasses
Magwitch: chains and manacles
Food for **Uncle Pumblechook**
Basin of water
Estella: keys
Jaggers: candle
Throne-like chair
Candles
Dressing-table. *On it*: dried flowers, jewels, prayer-book, pack of cards, cloth-
                covered mirror
Chair
Joe: pipe
Wet sponge for **Herbert**
Joe: indentures in hat
Book and pen for **Young Pip**
Sewing for **Biddy**
Jaggers: long purse with money
Pumblechook: small basket
Portmanteau for **Pip**
Brown paper parcel for **Young Pip**
High stool
Jaggers: brief
Herbert: paper bag of fruit
Table
Plates, tureen, cutlery
Chairs
Tea things
Note (in **Pip**'s dressing-gown pocket)

PART II

Small seat
Letter for **Herbert**
Villagers: umbrellas
Jaggers: silk handkerchief, watch
Bottle of port for **Molly**
Port glasses
Jaggers: banknote
Chair, toasting-fork, toast for **Aged Parent**
Union Jack
Small cannon
Table
Book for **Pip**
Lamp
Bottle of brandy, two glasses for **Pip**
Pip: purse containing two one-pound notes
Magwitch: open jack-knife
Pip: finger-ring
Prayer book
Lighted candles
Wemmick: small package containing sausage
Pip: invalid chair
Aged P: flower for buttonhole
Wemmick: ring
Pip: a book
Pumblechook: rice

LIGHTING PLOT

Practical fittings required: lamp
Composite set. Various interior and exterior settings

PART I

To open: Darkness

Cue 12	**Joe**: "That's what it is." *Cross-fade lights back to kitchen*	(Page 13)
Cue 13	**Pip**: "Next morning ..." *Cross-fade lights to exterior of* **Miss Havisham**'*s house*	(Page 14)
Cue 14	**Jaggers** appears with candle *Bring up covering spot on candle*	(Page 15)
Cue 15	**Jaggers** exits *Cut covering spot on candle*	(Page 15)
Cue 16	**Miss Havisham** comes into view with candles around her *Bring up covering spot on candles*	(Page 15)
Cue 17	**Estella** pushes **Pip** out *Cross-fade lights from* **Miss Havisham**'*s to forge kitchen*	(Page 18)
Cue 18	**Pip**: "... to feel ashamed of home." *Fade lights*	(Page 18)
Cue 19	When ready *Bring up light on* **Miss Havisham**'*s house*	(Page 18)
Cue 20	**Pip**: "I inwardly cry for her now." *Cross-fade lights to* **Miss Havisham**'*s room*	(Page 20)
Cue 21	**Mrs Joe** and **Pumblechook** enter the kitchen *Cross-fade lights to kitchen*	(Page 22)
Cue 22	**Pip**: " ... but once was not now." *Cross-fade lights from pub to* **Miss Havisham**'*s room,* *leaving spot on* **Pip**	(Page 24)
Cue 23	**Miss Havisham** exits *Fade lights on* **Miss Havisham**'*s room*	(Page 25)
Cue 24	**Pip**: " ... our part of the country ..." *Bring up light* DS	(Page 25)
Cue 25	**Biddy** tidies away **Mrs Joe**'s garments *Bring up lights on kitchen*	(Page 25)
Cue 26	**Pip** moves into the Satis House area *Bring up lights on* **Miss Havisham**'*s room*	(Page 29)
Cue 27	**Miss Havisham**: "And remember your benefactor." *Fade light on* **Miss Havisham**'*s room*	(Page 30)

| *Cue* 28 | **Pip** and **Young Pip** set off for London | (Page 32) |
| | *Cross-fade lights from* **Joe** *and* **Biddy** *to* **Wemmick** | |

| *Cue* 29 | **Pip** and **Herbert** go into their lodgings | (Page 34) |
| | *Cross-fade lights to the lodgings* | |

| *Cue* 30 | **Pip** reads his letter | (Page 36) |
| | *Bring up lights in forge area* | |

| *Cue* 31 | **Pip** crumples the letter | (Page 36) |
| | *Cross-fade from forge area to London area* | |

| *Cue* 32 | **Joe** moves to the kitchen | (Page 39) |
| | *Cross-fade lights to kitchen area* | |

PART II

| *To open*: | Darkness | |

| *Cue* 33 | When ready | (Page 40) |
| | *Bring up lights* c | |

| *Cue* 34 | **Young Pip**: " ... the larks sang high above it." | (Page 44) |
| | *Cross-fade lights to* **Miss Havisham**'s *area* | |

| *Cue* 35 | Post horn sounds | (Page 45) |
| | *Cross-fade lights to seat* DS | |

| *Cue* 36 | **Jaggers**: "Must my guests expire of sobriety?" | (Page 46) |
| | *Cross-fade lights to London area* | |

| *Cue* 37 | **Jaggers**: " ... is to be signed for." | (Page 49) |
| | *Fade lights on* **Jaggers**' *house, leaving* DS *area lit* | |

| *Cue* 38 | **Pip** stiffens, offended | (Page 50) |
| | *Cross-fade lights to* **Wemmick**'s *office* | |

| *Cue* 39 | **Pip** and **Wemmick** walk towards **Wemmick**'s home | (Page 51) |
| | *Slowly cross-fade lights from* **Wemmick**'s *office to* **Wemmick**'s *home, following* **Pip** *and* **Wemmick** | |

| *Cue* 40 | **Aged P.** : "Was that it, John? Did it go off?" | (Page 53) |
| | *Black-out* | |

| *Cue* 41 | Sound of wind and storm | (Page 53) |
| | *Bring up light on* **Young Pip** | |

Cue 42   **Young Pip**: " ... we no longer kept close company."   (Page 53)
*Bring up light on **Pip**'s rooms and practical lamp*

Cue 43   **Magwitch** places his jack-knife on the table   (Page 57)
*Cross-fade lights to **Jaggers'** room*

Cue 44   **Jaggers**: "Good-night, Pip."   (Page 57)
Cross-fade lights to Pip's rooms

Cue 45   **Herbert**: " ... Miss Havisham's lover ... "   (Page 58)
*Cross-fade lights to Satis House area; general cover
    with spots on candles*

Cue 46   **Estella**: "Here now, let us part friends."   (Page 60)
Bring up amber light US

Cue 47   **Estella**: *"Moth-er!"*   (Page 60)
Black-out

Cue 48   When ready   (Page 60)
*Bring up lights on **Wemmick**'s home*

Cue 49   **Jaggers** exits   (Page 63)
*Cross-fade lights to **Pip**'s lodgings*

Cue 50   **Pip**: "Yes. But no longer scowling."   (Page 64)
Cross-fade lights to small wharf and river

Cue 51   **Magwitch**: "Now I'm the world's master."   (Page 65)
Flash of lightning

Cue 52   Ship's siren sounds   (Page 65)
Cut lights on wharf; river remains lit

Cue 53   Siren sounds   (Page 65)
Flashes of lightning; black-out

Cue 54   Silence; when ready   (Page 66)
Bring up lights slowly

Cue 55   **Joe** stands beside **Biddy**   (Page 70)
Bring up light in Satis House area

EFFECTS PLOT

PART I

PART II

Cue 13	**Jaggers** and **Pip** sit *Post horn; whinnying of horses*	(Page 45)
Cue 14	**Young Pip**: "All passengers to coach!" *Post horn*	(Page 46)
Cue 15	**Jaggers**: "It is Havisham." *Post horn*	(Page 46)
Cue 156	**Herbert**: " — I truly do." *Carriage clock strikes the half hour*	(Page 49)
Cue 17	**Wemmick** lights the powder in the cannon *Great explosion and vast cloud of smoke*	(Page 53)
Cue 18	Lights go down; when ready *Sounds of wind and storm*	(Page 53)
Cue 19	Lights cross-fade to wharf *Fog swirls*	(Page 64)
Cue 20	Flash of lightning *Roll of thunder*	(Page 65)
Cue 21	**Pip** rows *Ship's siren sounds*	(Page 65)
Cue 22	**Magwitch**: "Compeyson!" *Siren*	(Page 65)
Cue 23	Flashes of lightning *Thunder*	(Page 65)
Cue 24	Black-out *Cut siren*	(Page 65)